BAD MAN DOWN

"You just keep talking," the gunman said with a grin that showed bloodstained teeth. "I know you're the one that killed one of our boys last night. You'll pay for that. You and all them women you keep in that fancy house."

Clint's eyes narrowed as he stared down at the gunman. Although he could easily spot the bluster in the other man's words, he knew there was some truth to them. Any longer in the open after all that shooting, and Clint would catch some lead himself.

"That's right," the gunman sneered, doing a good job of reading faces. "Keep on talking and you'll meet my friends. You'll get a real good look at 'em and then you can meet the devil, because that's where they'll send you."

"I think you might just have a point," Clint said.

The victorious smile on the gunman's face was short-lived. He felt a dull pain thump into the sore spot on the side of his head. From there, it was a quick drop into the blackness.

THE GUNSMITH
287
THE REAPERS

J. R. ROBERTS

JOVE BOOKS, NEW YORK

THE BERKLEY PUBLISHING GROUP
Published by the Penguin Group
Penguin Group (USA) Inc.
375 Hudson Street, New York, New York 10014, USA
Penguin Group (Canada), 90 Eglinton Avenue East, Suite 700, Toronto, Ontario M4P 2Y3, Canada
(a division of Pearson Penguin Canada Inc.)
Penguin Books Ltd., 80 Strand, London WC2R 0RL, England
Penguin Group Ireland, 25 St. Stephen's Green, Dublin 2, Ireland (a division of Penguin Books Ltd.)
Penguin Group (Australia), 250 Camberwell Road, Camberwell, Victoria 3124, Australia
(a division of Pearson Australia Group Pty. Ltd.)
Penguin Books India Pvt. Ltd., 11 Community Centre, Panchsheel Park, New Delhi—110 017, India
Penguin Group (NZ), Cnr. Airborne and Rosedale Roads, Albany, Auckland 1310, New Zealand
(a division of Pearson New Zealand Ltd.)
Penguin Books (South Africa) (Pty.) Ltd., 24 Sturdee Avenue, Rosebank, Johannesburg 2196,
South Africa

Penguin Books Ltd., Registered Offices: 80 Strand, London WC2R 0RL, England

This is a work of fiction. Names, characters, places, and incidents either are the product of the author's imagination or are used fictitiously, and any resemblance to actual persons, living or dead, business establishments, events, or locales is entirely coincidental.

THE REAPERS

A Jove Book / published by arrangement with the author

PRINTING HISTORY
Jove edition / November 2005

Copyright © 2005 by Robert J. Randisi.

ISBN: 0-515-14031-7

JOVE®
Jove Books are published by The Berkley Publishing Group,
a division of Penguin Group (USA) Inc.,
375 Hudson Street, New York, New York 10014.
JOVE is a registered trademark of Penguin Group (USA) Inc.
The "J" design is a trademark belonging to Penguin Group (USA) Inc.

PRINTED IN THE UNITED STATES OF AMERICA

10 9 8 7 6 5 4 3 2 1

ONE

It was quickly approaching dawn on a mild winter day. Of course, mild was a relative term for anyone. In this case, it meant that the wind wasn't blowing too hard and the cold wasn't bad enough to freeze every ounce of blood trying to make its way through a man's veins. At least that was the Nebraska definition of the word at that particular time.

Winters in Nebraska were a mixed bag. For the most part, they were long, brutal affairs that could test anyone's limits. They'd been the death of more travelers than could be counted if such folks found themselves in the middle of an unforgiving prairie without anything but a tarp and threadbare clothing to keep their skins warm.

Every now and then, the cold let up and the snows tapered off so someone might actually enjoy the sight of miles upon miles of white-dusted grass. On those days, the sun would shine off all that snow in a way that would make new shades of yellow and orange that seemed to be enhanced by the cold rather than hindered by it.

The cold was still there, to be sure. It seeped in underneath layers of coats and turned every breath into a smoky mist. It was the kind of cold that made nearly everything else in the world stop, as if to hold itself for warmth.

The air was still.

The animals were deep in their holes.

All that was left was a calm world and the few other things bold enough to disturb it.

Two men sat upon their horses, gazing out over this scene as their fingers clenched tightly around their reins. Although their breath swirled up in front of their faces, they weren't breaking the silence that only came with such a winter's day.

Both men had been looking on their own accord, simply letting their eyes wander where they might. At the moment, however, both men's eyes had become focused on the same spot in the distance. Neither of them wanted to say anything, partly because simply opening their mouths might allow a stray breeze to come in and sweep the breath straight from their lungs.

Indeed, "mild winter" was a relative term.

"You see that, Andy?" one of the riders asked.

The second man squinted into the distance before nodding. "Yeah. I see it."

The first man who'd spoken was Kyle Wrigley. Although most of his face was covered by a tattered wool scarf, the parts that could be seen were as chapped and weather-beaten as the saddle he sat upon. His eyes gazed out unblinkingly into the distance, fixed upon a target the way a circling hawk fixed upon a mouse.

Andy, the second man, was dressed in a similar fashion but was obviously less comfortable in the elements. The portion of his face that peeked up from his own scarf was so red that his desire to get back in front of a fire was easier to see than the horse under his legs.

"How many of them you think there are?" Andy asked.

Kyle narrowed his focus a bit more, pulled in a breath and let it out slowly. He gazed across the horizon at the shapes he'd spotted only moments ago. Despite the distance between them, Kyle swore he could hear echoes of the other riders' steps crunching against the snow.

"Looks like about four or five of them," Kyle finally replied. "Maybe more. It's hard to tell with the sun right behind them like that."

Shaking his head in frustration, Andy reached up to shield his eyes with an outstretched hand. "I hear that," he said, bumping his thumb against the brim of his hat. "Could be they're just passing through. In that case, there's probably not too many of them. They could be scouting ahead for a wagon train."

"At this time of year? I doubt it's any wagon train."

"It could be, though."

"Sure," Kyle replied under his breath. "It could be."

The older of the two riders knew that what he'd just said was true. It could very well have been a wagon train making its way across the plains on its way to California. Despite the time of year, there were still a few travelers who got a burr under their saddle so big that they risked all they had on a gamble like that one.

But the feeling in Kyle's gut told him something different. It told him that the riders he'd spotted weren't just scouts and they weren't just passing through. Although he didn't know exactly who the riders were, the possibilities that were left weren't too comforting. The fact that he was charged with guarding a swelling herd of cattle plumping themselves up for market didn't make Kyle feel much better.

"What should we do?" Andy asked. "You want me to head back and tell Hank?"

Kyle shook his head. "No need for that just yet. So far, we ain't seen anything but a few men on the horizon."

"Actually," Andy added, "make that a few more."

Sure enough, another pair of figures had come up beside the original few that had caught both men's attention. For a moment, all of the figures lined up like birds on a fence. Before Kyle could get a definite count, the figures turned and rode so they were no longer sticking out against the skyline.

Kyle didn't like this.

He still didn't have much more than a gut feeling, but he'd seen enough in his years to give that feeling a good amount of credence. "Tell you what. Why don't we get a closer look for ourselves before getting anyone else all riled up?"

Andy looked over to Kyle and back again. "Hank's been jumpy lately. This might be enough to get him to call out every gun he's got. On the other hand, that might not be a bad idea if those men are rustlers."

"They could also be a distraction," Kyle added. "If they're rustlers, they might be here to draw everyone off while another group sneaks in to help themselves to some beef."

The tension in Andy's face was plain to see no matter how many times his scarf had been wrapped around his head. His eyes and manner had taken on a stiffness that had nothing at all to do with the cold.

Sensing this immediately, Kyle said, "Or they could still be scouts for some wagon train that likes the damn cold. Why don't we figure out which it is before kicking up too much dust? How's that sound?"

"Sounds good to me," Andy said, responding to the easiness in Kyle's tone. "I'll ride up and around to the left and you can take the right."

Kyle nodded. "Keep your distance and keep your eyes open. Don't get too close. Just get a look and head back to this spot. Quick and easy."

Pulling in a lungful of cold air, Andy held it for as long as he could bear before letting it out in a gust of steam. With that, he snapped his reins and headed off in the direction he'd announced moments ago.

Kyle watched the younger man head off, satisfied that Andy was taking a path wide enough to keep some distance between himself and whoever else was out there. He then brought his own horse to face the proper direction and flicked the leather straps over his animal's back.

The horse took a few steps to get the blood flowing before breaking into a full run.

Knowing his horse would go where it was told, Kyle took his eyes from the road ahead and glanced back at the horizon where the figures had been. Not only were they no longer there, but there wasn't so much as a trace of them to be seen. Considering how flat the land was, that meant that those riders wanted to get out of sight and had done so in seconds.

That feeling crept back into Kyle's gut.

He didn't like this one bit.

TWO

The Double Briar Ranch was situated on a fine piece of land in western Nebraska. The closest town was a modest place named Flat Rock, which wasn't exactly too close to much of anything else. It was the kind of place that just as many folks found themselves stuck in as they did settled there. Even so, the Double Briar had done nothing but grow since it had been built.

That prosperity was due mostly to the owner of the ranch. He was a squat man with a face full of thick bristles which wouldn't be shaved off until well into the spring. Hank Ossutt had built the ranch house and put up most of the fence surrounding his property. His men were hand-picked and damn close to family in his eyes.

One of those men was coming back now, thundering in from the front twenty as if he could already smell the steaks that were being cooked up for supper. Hank stood on his porch with his arms crossed. Once the rider got a little closer, he stepped down onto the packed earth and waited for the horse to be reined in.

"Jesus Christ," Hank said as he walked forward to greet the newly arrived man. "For a moment there, I thought you might ride straight into the cookhouse." Taking a moment to get a look at who was on the horse in front of him, Hank started glancing behind the other man. "What's the matter, Kyle? You lose Andy?"

"You mean he's not here?" Kyle asked.

Hank took another look around and shook his head. "I haven't seen him, but that don't mean he's not kicking around here someplace."

"I'll check around."

Hank's eyes narrowed and he stepped forward quickly enough to take hold of Kyle's reins. More than able to control the horse with one hand, Hank focused on Kyle's face. "Something's wrong."

As much as he wanted to brush off those words, Kyle knew better than to think he could do so too easily under Hank's intense stare. "Could be. I don't know just yet."

"Did something happen out there? Was Andy hurt?"

"We spotted some riders on the edge of the property line and split up to get a look."

"Andy's the new man, you should know better than to—"

"We just split to take a quick peek and come back again. We weren't apart for more than a few minutes. Hell, the ones I spotted weren't even close enough to wave at me and Andy was giving them a wider berth than I was."

Hank nodded and let go of the reins. Instead, he patted the horse's nose and took some of the edge from his own voice. "You saw some riders?"

"Yeah. Less than a dozen, but not by much. I wasn't able to get too good a look at them. Like I said, I wanted to make it a quick peek before leaving Andy on his own for too long."

"Were the riders armed?"

"They weren't waving guns over their head, but that's all I would have seen from where I was. They had the sun to their backs."

"Well that shouldn't be a problem anymore," Hank said, glancing up at the sky, which had darkened to a soft shade of purple. "I didn't hear anything from any of the others on patrol, so Andy probably fell and busted his leg or something."

"I thought he might have come back here, so I'll still ask around right quick before heading out again."

"Sounds fine. And Kyle," Hank added before the other man got too far away.

Having already flicked his reins and gotten his horse moving, Kyle looked back down to the burly ranch owner who was wrapped in a thick leather coat stuffed with sheepskin. Hank Ossutt looked as gnarled and tough as some of the stumps that had required a team of mules to pull out of the ground when the house was being built. "Yeah?"

"Take some of the other boys with you."

"That might not be necessary. I'll just—"

"You'll just do what I say," Hank cut in sharply. "No need to take 'em all. Just take a few out for a ride, ask them to follow you out when you go looking for Andy. If Andy did got pitched from his horse, he'll need more than you to drag him back."

"True enough." Without wanting to waste another second, Kyle nodded and turned his back to the rancher.

Hank watched just long enough to see that Kyle was heading where he said he'd be going. From there, Hank turned toward the house and stomped inside. No more than three or four of his steps thumped into the front part of the house before some of the people inside reacted.

One of the first to come into Hank's sight was a young brunette wearing a light gray dress and a matching shawl about her shoulders. "What's wrong, Daddy?"

"Nothing's wrong, Lynne. Get back to what you were doing."

"You're stomping like a bull in there," she said as she emerged from the adjoining room, wincing at the cold air blowing in from outside. "Did that fence break again? I told you to let the others patch it up instead of you doing it all by yourself. If you don't let someone help, you'll—"

Hank shot a quick glance over to the girl that was full of enough venom to stop her in her tracks. "I told you it's fine!"

Despite the fact that she was in her early twenties, the brunette recoiled from those words like a child who'd been rapped on the top of her head. The look in her eyes lasted for a second or two before being replaced by an anger more befitting her age.

"I own a piece of this ranch too, you know," Lynne said. "And that means I need to know about what goes on here. Now what's the commotion about?"

Hank forced himself to calm down a bit as he stepped forward to take hold of his daughter by the shoulders. His grip was firm, yet reassuring as he rubbed her arms while also moving her back into the room from which she'd come.

"Looks like Andy might have taken a fall," Hank said. "And we might be having some visitors for a late supper."

"Is that all?"

"So far, it is."

Letting out a little, huffing breath, Lynne said, "I hope Andy's all right. How many might be coming for dinner?"

"I don't know yet. Maybe none. That's what Kyle's riding out to see."

After a moment, the brunette shrugged and patted her father on the shoulder. "You shouldn't get so worked up about every little thing," she said before placing a little kiss on Hank's cheek. "It'll be the death of you."

Hank nodded and watched as his daughter turned and walked back into the next room. The smells of supper being prepared wafted through the house, reminding him of everything he'd built up for himself in the form of the Double Briar Ranch.

In the time since he'd sunken his first fence post, there

had been plenty of men out to take what was his. Between competition from other ranchers and dealing with the criminals laying in wait along every trail from Omaha to Texas, Hank and his men had done a lot of fighting.

That didn't make him any different from plenty of other ranchers. It just made him wary of the world in general and even more protective of what was his.

"Percy," Hank called out.

"Yes, sir?" a blonde replied after rushing out from the dining room.

"Send word to some of those new men I just hired on. Tell them to meet up with Kyle and lend him a hand."

The blonde's hands were filled with silverware, which she quickly dropped into the pocket on the front of the apron tied around her waist. "I think some of them are just coming in for supper."

"Good. Make sure they get out and saddled up right away."

THREE

Kyle wasn't surprised by the fact that nobody he talked to had seen Andy since both of them had ridden out on their patrol hours ago. As he'd been instructed, Kyle asked each man to saddle up and come with him until there was a group of four other men riding behind him.

Before he could head away from the cluster of buildings at the center of the ranch, Kyle was stopped by another group galloping up to meet him.

"What the hell is this?" Kyle asked. Although he recognized all of the faces around him, Kyle wasn't exactly pleased to see all of them so close. "I've got the men I need. The rest of you can go back to what you were doing."

"Mr. Ossutt told us to come along with you," one of the men in the other group said.

"What for?"

"I don't know. The boss tells us to ride out with you, so that's what we're doing."

Kyle looked over the faces of the men in the second group. As far as he knew, they were all good enough workers, but most of them had only been working at the Double Briar for a month or less.

"I don't need all of you," Kyle said. "If there's rustlers

out there, they'll see us coming a mile away. If Andy's just got a busted leg or something, this is unnecessary."

"Orders are orders."

Kyle could see that he wasn't about to get through such a simple line of reasoning, especially since the man who'd given those orders was the same one who put the food on the table every night. Rather than try to swim upstream, Kyle snapped his reins and got the entire convoy moving out the front gates of the homestead.

The sound of all those horses became a low grumble in the cold quiet of the early evening. As their steps fell into unison, that grumble became a thunder which hung in the air like a storm. With a smirk on his face, Kyle touched his heels to his horse's sides to get the animal to pour on that last bit of steam.

Sure enough, the horse responded and launched into a gallop that left a good portion of the others behind. Of the ones who could catch up, only a few were from the new men, which suited Kyle just fine.

The land sprawled out in front of him like an unmade bed. It was flat for the most part, with several lumps and a few sizeable rises to break things up. Even with so much spread out before him, Kyle knew there was plenty of room for surprises along the way. If men didn't want to be seen, there were ways to go about unnoticed and move where they weren't wanted.

Kyle had seen the riders do a good job of disappearing not too long ago. Although that didn't make them trouble, it didn't do any good for that feeling in his gut either. Without taking the time to stop and give directions, Kyle led by example and headed toward the last spot where Andy should have been.

Once they got to the spot where he and Andy had parted ways, Kyle brought the group to a stop and turned to get a look at who was left. Just as he'd figured, the men he'd asked to come along were able to keep up. The few others who'd stayed the course had also managed to earn a few points of respect in Kyle's eyes.

"Andy was supposed to meet me right here," Kyle said. "If he's hurt, he'll try to get back here if he can't make it to the house."

"Or he could be somewhere in between," one of the newer men spoke up. "There's a good couple of miles to cover between here and there."

"Right," Kyle said. "Why don't you search the area in between while me and the others head forward?" With that, Kyle brought his horse around and motioned for his own select group to follow.

The newer man who'd spoken up looked at one of the other faces who'd been part of that second group. Although this man was one of the few who'd kept up with Kyle and his original selection, the look on his face made it seem as if he'd done all the running instead of his horse.

"You heard him," the first of the new men said. "Head back and search the area between here and the house. Take the others with you."

The relief on the second man's face was easy enough to see as he tipped his hat and brought his horse around to face in the opposite direction. From there, he snapped the reins and rode off to round up the others who'd either been too slow or too nervous to keep up in the first place.

"Jesus," he grunted under his breath. "I didn't sign up for this."

FOUR

Kyle and one other man were at a stop in a remote corner of Ossutt's land. They were close to the fence line and not much else, and wooden rails stretched out as far as the eye could see in front or behind them. With the sun almost gone completely, the cold was taking a firm grip on the air, as well as anyone foolish enough to be out in it.

Hearing the sound of an approaching horse, Kyle shifted in his saddle to get a look at the source. When he saw who was making the noise, he shifted back around again and waited until the steps came to a stop beside him.

"What are you doing here?" Kyle asked. "I thought I told you to search the area closer to home."

The new man settled in his saddle, peering at the same spot that seemed to be drawing everyone else's attention. "I had the other men see to it. I doubt they'd be good for much else."

"Not very kind words for your partners."

"No offense meant. They just looked a bit skittish to me, is all."

The man at Kyle's other side chuckled under his breath. "Skittish. That's a kinder word than I would've used."

Kyle gave the new man a closer look, nodded and then

14

turned back to what he'd been looking at before. The moves were subtle, but the man's bearing changed noticeably from one glance to another. For the moment, the new man seemed to have been accepted by the rest.

For the moment.

"There's some movement down there," Kyle said, nodding in the direction where everyone was staring. "You see it?"

"Yeah. Three riders. Maybe four."

"I'll be damned," Kyle's partner said. "I didn't make out that fourth one until just now."

"Quiet down, Mace," Kyle scolded.

Mace looked over to the new man and gave him an exaggerated shrug.

If Kyle noticed the exchange, he didn't give any indication. Instead, he lowered his own voice even more while lowering his head like a wolf setting its sights upon its prey. "Those men are crowded around that fence just like the ones me and Andy spotted earlier. If'n they're not the same ones, I'll bet they know where them others are."

"And if they are the same ones?" Mace asked.

"Then I want to have a word with them all the same." Looking over to the newest member of his group, Kyle said, "You sure you're up for this?"

"They could just be passing through and waiting to see if anyone will give them a proper greeting," the new man said.

Kyle nodded warily. "And they could be ready to draw on us if we get too close. It might be nothing or it might get rough."

"I made it this far. I might as well see it through."

"Suit yourself." With that, Kyle snapped his reins and rode forward. Mace followed close behind.

All three men headed straight toward the group gathered at the fence, knowing full well that they weren't going to be able to hide on the flat stretch of open land. They were a

few bluffs here and there, but nothing in the area where
Kyle had been waiting. The only thing in his favor had
been the darkness, but that wasn't thick enough to keep
him and the other two hidden once they started moving toward the fence.

As Kyle and the other two got closer, the four men gathered near the fence shifted so they were facing them directly. There were still no weapons in plain sight, but their
posture and mannerisms became more and more defensive
as the two groups got closer.

By the time Kyle drew to a stop, the groups were close
enough to see the steam coming from one another's mouth.
There was a chill in the air that had nothing to do with the
season and each man's eyes had taken on a hard, steely
glint.

"This here is private property," Kyle announced.

There were four men in the group. Now that they were
close enough, Kyle and the other two could plainly see the
holsters strapped around the waists of the other men. At
least two of those men had rifles holstered to their saddles
as well. For the moment, none of the guns had cleared
leather.

For the moment.

"We're on the proper side of the fence," one of the men
at the middle of the four said. "There's no law against that."

The tone in Kyle's voice was calm, but tempered with
enough of an edge to make it known that he meant business. "Nobody said you were breaking any laws. I was just
making sure you knew where you stood."

"We're standing on this side of your fence. On the other
side is the Double Briar Ranch. We saw the sign a ways
down the line well enough."

"Then do you mind stating your business here? If it's
food or shelter you're after, we can talk to the owner of this
spread for you. He's not against lending a helping hand
when it's needed."

"That'd be appreciated."

"Where's the rest of your men?"

"Pardon me?"

The air had taken on a sudden chill as the spokesman for the group across the fence locked eyes with Kyle in a manner that was just short of a challenge.

Mace leaned forward in his saddle and spoke up. "There were others spotted not too far from here, nosing up close to the property line just like you men here. It seems safe to say that you're all part of the same group."

"And what if we are?"

"Then it would be good for us to know so there's no words spoken out of turn between them and the rest of our men," Mace said. "It'd be best to keep things nice and civil like we've got right here."

The man who'd done the talking for the group of four looked at Mace, Kyle and the new man in turn. The corners of his mouth curled up in an amused grin that looked like it had been taken from the face of a coyote. "Don't worry about them," he said. "I'd say you boys got more than you can handle right here."

And in that moment, the coyote bared his fangs.

FIVE

The man who'd been doing the talking for the group of four behind the fence was the first one to go for his gun. The other three weren't too far behind him, however, and managed to clear leather in the span of one second.

When that first move toward a gun was taken, Kyle reacted as best he could. All the while, he cursed himself for being in this situation in the first place. Even as his hand slapped against the grip of his pistol, he knew he'd be unable to draw before the first shot was fired at him.

Thunder roared from the first gun barrel, spitting a gout of sparks from the spokesman for the group of four. In the growing darkness, the shot blasted like a flicker of sunlight followed by the stench of burnt powder.

Three more shots peppered the air after that first. Two of them came from the group on the other side of the fence while another came from one of the men behind Kyle. More shots crackled through the air, turning the entire scene into a chaotic jumble of sound and fury.

Lead hissed past Kyle's face, and another piece chewed into his leg. The horse beneath him let out a pained whinny and started to rear up onto its hind legs. Kyle's gun was in hand and he squeezed off a shot at the other four men.

Although he knew he was way off the mark, he did see one of the other four get knocked from his saddle like a target getting dropped in a shooting gallery. Blood sprayed out behind him, looking like a black mist in the shadows.

Reflexively, Kyle looked behind him and saw that both Mace and the new man had their guns drawn. Mace was gripping his reins, doing his best to keep his horse from bolting, while firing shot after shot toward the men at the fence.

The new man was keeping low in the saddle, positioning himself somewhere out of the immediate line of fire. As he moved, he squeezed off a few rounds of his own. Kyle was just glad that his backup hadn't up and run when things turned to hell.

Only a second or two had passed, but it felt like an eternity since the last time Kyle had taken a look at the other four men. Of those four, only three remained in their saddles. One of those was wobbling and holding onto his side. That didn't stop him from taking aim at Kyle, however.

Before he knew what he was doing, Kyle had lifted his gun and pulled the trigger. Another shot roared from behind him as the man who'd been about to put him down was rocked in his saddle in a gruesome dance.

First, a flap of skin erupted from his hip, twisting him around until one of his legs almost flipped up and over his horse's rump. Then, another hole was punched open as the second round drilled through his chest. Oddly enough, that impact seemed to right his balance and straighten the man up in his saddle.

In a moment that seemed to take place independent of everything else going on, the man on the other side of the fence blinked his eyes and took a long look at Kyle and the two men beside him. His mouth opened, but any sound that he might have made was swallowed up by the thunder of gunfire.

At first, the man looked like he was going to fall for-

ward onto his saddle horn. The black wound in his chest
started to glisten as more blood seeped into his shirt. His
eyes then rolled up into his head and he flopped over onto
his back. The only thing that kept him from falling off his
horse completely was the fact that his feet were still firmly
wedged into his stirrups.

At that moment, everything else snapped into focus and
Kyle was able to focus back on what was going on. Some-
how, he'd managed to empty his pistol and had forced the
other men far enough back that he had a little more room
and just enough time to take a breath.

"Head out!"

The words roared through the air in much the same way
that the lead had been doing over the last few seconds.
And, much like that lead, they had an immediate impact on
those for whom they were intended.

The men on the other side of the fence backed up but
didn't stop firing. Two of them reached out to take hold of
the reins of other horses while the man who'd been the
only one among them to speak pulled a second gun from
where it had been holstered.

Clearing the saddle holster in a single sweep, the shotgun reared its head like a venomous snake. It was placed
against the spokesman's shoulder and brought to bear upon
Kyle and his two partners.

"Scatter!" was all Kyle could think to say once he saw
what was about to happen.

Fortunately for everyone involved, Kyle and the other
two men did precisely that. They scattered like leaves in a
breeze moments before the shotgun unleashed its own fury
in the form of a thundering roar.

Smoke and lead blazed through the air, shredding skin,
leather, clothing and anything else it came across. As that
single, deafening blast rolled into a distant echo, the smoke
descended like a gritty black shroud.

Kyle still gripped his pistol even though he knew it

wasn't much more than a useless weight in his hand. His eyes darted around to try and catch sight of the two men that had been at his side. With the smell of blood thick in the air, he prayed to the Lord that none of it belonged to his friends.

"Mace?" Kyle shouted over the ringing in his ears. "Mace, where are you?"

After a few terrible moments, Kyle finally heard the voice he'd been hoping for.

"Right here," Mace replied. Sure enough, the big man was wincing and clearing his throat no more than a few yards from where Kyle's horse was standing. "What about that other one?"

Kyle was already looking around for the new man who'd joined his little group. The longer it took to find him, the more Kyle cursed himself for going against his better judgment. Although he didn't know the fellow as much more than a slightly familiar face, he didn't exactly want the man's death on his conscience either.

Just as dread was starting to settle firmly in his gut, he shifted his eyes back toward the fence where the shooting had taken place. Sure enough, there was one figure on horseback there looking over the fence where the group of four had been standing. The new man was clearing his throat while sliding fresh rounds into the cylinder of his pistol.

"You all right?" Kyle asked.

The new man looked over at him and nodded. "A little scratched from some of that shotgun blast, but nothing too bad. How about you two?"

Kyle was already looking back in Mace's direction. "I'm fine. What about you, Mace? Looks like you caught one or two back there."

Mace was holding his left side. He kept that same arm pressed tightly against him while nodding. "Looks worse than it is. Can't say the same for them two."

Both of the others looked to where Mace was pointing. On the ground on the other side of the fence was one body and a mess of blood. Although the body wasn't the source of all the blood, it was laying too awkwardly and too still to be anything but a dead husk.

"There was another that was killed," Mace said. "Looked to me like he got dragged by his horse."

There was a haunted look in Kyle's eyes as he said, "Yeah. I saw that happen, too." Shaking his head slightly, he turned to look into the eyes of the new man. "You did real good, mister. I never did catch your name."

The new man reached out to shake the hand Kyle offered. "The name's Clint."

SIX

Clint had meant to pass through Nebraska and make his way into California over the next few weeks. It was a loose plan, but those were the only ones he could ever seem to afford. Although the winter months were tightening their grip over most of the country, California was usually able to shake free of that icy grasp.

As always, things had a tendency to find Clint no matter where he was or where he was headed. This time was no different and the things that had found him weren't particularly good.

During a brief stay in Omaha, Clint had heard rumors about a gang of thieves cutting a bloody trail through Nebraska and Kansas. According to the stories, the gang would do their damage in one state and then seek refuge in the other. Once the commotion had died down, they would start over again.

Clint knew enough lawmen in the area to confirm some of those stories and his instincts fleshed out a few more. He'd spent enough time tracking down outlaws that he could easily follow their line of thought. From what he could tell, this gang did exist and they were operating in the general pattern that he'd heard.

Of course, just how vicious the gang was and how many men they'd killed made up the bulk of the stories told about them. Because of that, Clint figured he'd never really know that part for certain.

Then again, the one thing that was in Clint's favor was that he wasn't a lawman himself. Therefore, matters that weren't his problem could be shucked off like a coat on a warm day. There were plenty of gangs out there, and it wasn't his business to track every last one of them down. Even the lawmen that he knew were smart enough to keep from getting too obsessed about hunting down every last one of those animals on their own. There would always be plenty to go around, and so far, Clint hadn't even crossed paths with one of this supposed gang.

Having made it almost through Nebraska, Clint had found himself in an unusual spot. He wasn't exactly lost, but he ran into a string of bad luck where his knowledge of the local geography was concerned.

East of the Mississippi River, most towns were well established enough to have roots more than a foot deep. Traveling west, on the other hand, was a different story. Towns came and went at the whim of some very fickle mistresses.

Gold towns sprouted at the first sight of a shiny rock and blew away as soon as that shine faded. There were coal mining towns that could collapse as quickly as a deep tunnel and even guano towns that broke apart as quickly as the groups of bats that had brought them there.

A man traveling west would see no end of things to make him shake his head in wonder. Even a man as experienced as Clint Adams was sometimes caught by surprise. One such instance had happened when he'd ridden into his fourth town in a row that was nothing more than empty streets and a few empty, crumbling shacks.

The first few hadn't been too surprising and had served as a better campsite than the middle of an open stretch of prairie. The next one had gotten Clint annoyed since he'd been looking forward to sleeping on a real bed and getting some real cooking in his belly.

And the fourth ghost town had been a real problem. By the time Clint had ridden into that one, his supplies were getting low and Eclipse was getting awfully wary. Somewhere along the trail, the Darley Arabian stallion had thrown a shoe. Although the horse was doing an admirable job of getting Clint where he needed to go, there was only so much that could be expected of any animal.

Clint had had his fat pulled from the fire by the stallion more times than he could count and wasn't about to return the favor by putting the horse's health at stake. One bad stretch of road, a misplaced nail in the road or any number of little disasters could put Eclipse into a world of hurt. For that reason, more than any of the others, Clint would have wagered his last dollar in hopes that the town of Ambling Creek was still up and running.

He would have lost.

Ambling Creek was the worst of the lot, partly because the town had fallen into a half-assed collection of old lumber arranged in a sloppy row. Most of the disappointment came from the fact that Clint was truly hoping against hope to find some civilization.

It was an odd feeling. Although he could have survived for months living off the land under normal circumstances, these weren't exactly normal. Eclipse was in need of a blacksmith; Clint was in need of a hotel and restaurant and his saddlebags were in need of a general store.

Not exactly one to be caught off his guard, Clint had cinched his belt tight and made it his mission to get all those needs tended to. Eclipse had been through far worse and was always ready to step up to anything that was thrown at him.

Once Clint had abandoned everything he'd thought he knew about the area, he started looking for hard evidence of what was truly there. In less than two days, he caught sight of a well-worn trail leading off the main path. Following that, he spotted a fence that was in better shape than any of the man-made structures he'd seen in a good, long while.

Fences didn't build themselves, and tended to be the first things to go once there was nobody left to tend them. In no time at all, Clint made his way onto the Double Briar Ranch. The owner was a burly, older fellow by the name of Hank Ossutt.

Hank had the rugged build and harsh eyes that most landowners tended to get. Beneath that, however, was a warm heart and a giving soul. After a hot meal and a little conversation, Hank not only offered Clint a bed for the night, but also offered him a job.

It had been a hell of a long time since he'd worked as a ranch hand, but a little honest labor never hurt anyone. In fact, it seemed like a nice change from the normal business of finding a town and doing his best to keep from attracting the attention of young guns looking to prove themselves by outdrawing The Gunsmith.

When he saw that Ossutt had a blacksmith on his property, it made the prospect of staying there for a while even better. When he'd caught a glimpse of Ossutt's daughter, Clint knew he'd found the right place.

Then, right when he was getting comfortable in his routine, Clint was mustered to help look for a man lost on the property. That's when he got the familiar taste of gunpowder in the back of his throat, and his hands on the grip of his modified Colt.

At that moment, Clint wondered if he was some kind of lightning rod for trouble. No time to dwell on that just then. He had work to do.

SEVEN

Once he'd reloaded the Colt, Clint dropped it back into its holster and brought Eclipse around to face Kyle and Mace. Kyle looked rattled, but not overly so. Apart from the smudges of black powder on his face, there weren't any marks on him.

Mace looked to be in worse shape. The man had a look about him that reminded Clint of an old, petrified tree trunk. It had obviously been around for a long time, but was too tough to be uprooted anytime soon. His face was covered with an uneven layer of gray whiskers that looked more like a mat rather than any sort of beard. When he pressed his hand to his side, a wince twisted his mouth and brow.

"You all right?" Clint asked.

Mace sucked in a breath and nodded. Sitting up straight in his saddle, he said, "Just a nick, is all. Feels like it clipped a rib." Using his thumb and first two fingers, he pushed through the bloody tear in his coat and shirt.

Just watching Mace dig around in the wound on his side was enough to make Clint wince. He swore he could feel the jabs of pain that had to be slicing through Mace's torso.

In fact, it seemed that Clint and Kyle could feel it more than Mace himself.

"Yeah," Mace grunted as he pulled his hand up and showed the bloody fingers to the other two. "Just a nick. That bullet might've chipped a rib, but it made it through nice and clean."

Nice and clean weren't exactly the words Clint might have come up with at that moment, but it seemed to do well enough. He was just glad that Mace was through prodding the bloody hole in his side.

Kyle let out a breath and said, "Why don't you head back and get that side tended to? Clint and I can take it from here."

"You sure about that?" Mace asked. "Those assholes might come back to finish what they started."

"Those assholes took heavier casualties than we did," Clint pointed out. "I'm pretty sure they are finished for the night."

After seeing a nod from Kyle, Mace allowed himself to slump a bit in his saddle. "I guess you're right. I'll go check on them others and see if they found Andy yet. You think they got into a scrape like this one?"

Kyle glanced over his shoulder even though he couldn't see much of anything through the thick shadows that had fallen. "If they had, we would've heard the shots." Suddenly, his brow furrowed and he squinted even harder into the distance. "They must have heard these shots. Either those others have less guts than I thought or they did run into some trouble."

"I'll go check on 'em," Mace said. "And before you say anything, I'll be sure to let you know if I spot anything peculiar. First sign of trouble, I'll fire a shot into the air."

"Fine," Kyle said. "We won't be here long anyhow."

With that, Mace snapped his reins and got his horse running back along the path toward the house. When Kyle shifted his eyes toward Clint, he saw that Eclipse's saddle was already empty and Clint was on the ground on the other side of the fence. Kyle climbed down and joined Clint at the bloody patch of earth.

Clint squatted down to get himself as close as he could to the ground without getting on his knees. The tips of his fingers drifted over the wet spots at his feet and his eyes tracked a few inches ahead of them.

"You see anything?" Kyle asked.

"Just enough to tell me that we killed two of those men instead of just the one here. With all this blood, if that second one isn't dead already, he soon will be. That is, unless a third one was hit in this same spot."

Kyle's eyes glazed over for a moment as he saw the man flop forward and back in his saddle after getting shot. When he blinked, he found Clint looking back at him with a similar expression.

"It was just that one other," Kyle said. "You know that just as well as I do."

"Really?" Clint asked in a testing manner.

Kyle nodded. "Because you were the one who put him down."

Clint wiped his hands upon a clean patch of ground before standing up and dusting his hands on his hip.

"I saw you do it," Kyle continued. "I mean, I know I hit him too, but I wasn't the one to put him down for good. That shot had to have come from you, and if you hadn't done it, I wouldn't be standing here right now."

Although Clint didn't acknowledge those words directly, he didn't deny them either. "You were holding your own just fine. Especially considering that we were all caught in a bad spot."

"But you were quicker to act than anyone else. If you hadn't returned fire so fast, Mace and me would have been lying here in the dirt right next to that man there."

Clint saw the look in Kyle's eyes. It wasn't the first time he'd seen that look, either. There was a mix of respect and fear on Kyle's face, and it wasn't easy to pin down which part was stronger than the other. As the memories rushed through Kyle's head, the balance kept tipping from one side to another.

For the moment, the balance tipped a bit more toward respect, and Kyle straightened up. "We're not going to find much of anything in the dark. We'd best head back to make sure the others didn't run into any trouble of their own."

"Maybe we should get a fire going," Clint offered. "Make a few torches. Anything to get some light so we can see what there is to see while we're here."

Kyle was already on his horse and moving away. With a dismissive wave over his shoulder he said, "This place is a mess and it'll still be a mess come first light. If there's anything to find, I'll be able to find it then."

"Even if someone comes along to cover their tracks?"

"They'd have to know this property better than me, so yeah—even if they try to cover their tracks, they won't get 'em all."

Clint paused where he was and took another look at the ground near his feet.

"Come on, Clint," Kyle called out. "Trust me on this one."

Deciding to do just that, Clint made his way back to where Eclipse was waiting and climbed into the saddle.

EIGHT

The ride back was about twice as long as the first trip, but was less than half as interesting. Clint followed a bit behind and to the side of Kyle so the other man could lead the way along the path he wanted to search. They covered a meandering trail which eventually brought them right back to the house situated at the middle of Ossutt's land.

Throughout the ride back, the skies became a thick, velvety black and the air got so cold that it made every breath pinch inside Clint's lungs. With the growing chill in the air, the sounds of the horses' steps became that much louder. It also made it that much harder to keep their eyes open as the biting winds threatened to freeze their eyelids in place.

Despite all of that, both men persevered and checked out every bit of land that Kyle wanted to cover. The only thing they got for their efforts was a chill that went straight down to the bone.

Andy was nowhere to be found and neither were any of the others.

As they rode through the front gates of the homestead, Clint and Kyle were starting to feel more than the cold in the air. Although the wounds they'd sustained during the

31

fight were anything but serious, they were nagging at both of them like chiggers under their clothes.

Every so often, Clint would reach around to test a sore spot and find a deep scratch which had come from being grazed by a passing bit of lead. Between all the pistol rounds and that shotgun blast, it was hard to say exactly where the nicks had come from. All that mattered was that there was nothing to worry about.

Indeed, there were much bigger things to worry about at the moment.

"Where the hell have you been?" Hank Ossutt asked as he came stomping down from the front porch of his house. "I was just about to send all the boys back out to find you!"

Kyle ignored the rancher's barrage of words for the moment as he looked around at all the faces in the vicinity. "Where's Mace? Did he come back yet?"

"Sure he did, along with the rest."

"Along with Andy?"

"No," Ossutt replied with a sigh. "Not him."

The blonde who did most of the work inside Ossutt's home was crouched down at one end of the porch. When she stood up to look over at Kyle and Hank, she moved enough to show that she'd been crouching over one of the very subjects of the current conversation.

Mace was sitting with his back against a post. His jacket was open and his shirt was rolled up just high enough to reveal the bloody wound in his side. "About time you two got back," he said. "I've been meaning to get back out there and bring you in before Percy here got ahold of me."

The blond maid looked over at Clint and kept her eyes on him for a few seconds. Only when she saw that he was all right did she shift her attention back to the man sitting on the porch. "Now that you've seen them for yourself, do you think you can get inside? I won't have you freezing out here like some kind of fool."

"I'll be fine," Mace said as he pulled himself onto his

feet. "If all that shooting couldn't finish me, then a bit of cold won't hurt." Despite his grumbling, Mace pulled his jacket around him and walked into the house.

Some of the younger boys working at the Double Briar ran over to take the reins from Clint and Kyle as they dropped down from their saddles. In no time at all, the horses were led to the stables and Ossutt himself was approaching the men.

"What the hell happened out there?" the rancher asked. "I tried to get the story from Mace, but he wouldn't say much of anything apart from wanting to ride back out and find you two."

"What about the others?" Kyle asked.

"They heard the shooting, but didn't run into any trouble themselves."

"No. I mean did any of them get hurt?"

"Take a breath, Kyle. I just said they didn't run into any trouble." Resting an arm around Kyle's shoulder, Hank looked at the others milling about the front of the house. "Will someone fetch these men some coffee? Or how about some whiskey? Maybe that would do you more good."

"Coffee's fine for me," Clint said quickly.

"Same here."

"Get some coffee!" Hank bellowed. "Pronto!"

Kyle was distracted until he was able to set his eyes upon every last man who'd gone out to search for Andy. Once he saw for himself that they were all back and in good condition, he allowed his shoulders to come down from around his ears.

NINE

While checking on his own to see if there were any casualties, Clint got a good taste of just how closely knit everyone was. All the workers, right down to the new men who'd signed on after Clint had arrived, were treated like family. It wasn't until he'd made sure everyone was safe and accounted for that Hank allowed himself to take a seat.

The rancher took the cup of steaming coffee from the blond maid and helped himself to a quick sip. "Thanks, Percy."

Nodding gently, the maid extended the tray she was holding to the other three men seated in the corner of Hank's study. Mace had the best seat in the house and was sitting in a chaise lounge with bandages wrapped around his midsection and one leg propped up on the padding. Clint and Kyle were both sitting in straight-backed chairs that were built more for decoration than comfort, while Hank sat in a chair covered in dark red, velvet cushions.

"All right," Hank said as he wrapped his hand around the steaming cup. "Everyone's here. We're all accounted for. Now I want to hear about what the hell went on out there tonight."

Kyle spoke up right away, giving the rancher a fairly detailed account of what had gone on when he and Andy had first spotted the figures gathered by the fence. He then went on to fill in the specifics about everything that had taken place after that, including meeting up with the other ranch hands and finding the second group of strangers.

At this point, Hank took a particular interest. He listened to every last word describing the encounter and the gunfight that had followed. Every now and then he would nod, but mostly he just let Kyle tell the story however he wanted.

Although the account was a bit sparse here and there, it covered all the important points. When he was finished, Kyle took the first sip of his coffee and asked, "What did you hear from the others?"

"Nothing half as exciting as all that. Just that there was some shooting and they wanted to know what to do about it." Lowering his voice, Hank added, "I wanted to tell them they should have gone to help you right away, but it was too late for that. Truth be told, I'm not sure how much good they would have been for you in a spot like that."

"I can agree to that," Mace said without bothering to lower his voice. "They're good boys, but they ain't never been under fire like that. Any of them tells you different, and they're just blowing smoke." When he said that last part, Mace glanced over to one of the young faces looking in on them from another room.

Clint recognized that younger face as one of the men who'd been sent out with him to lend Kyle a hand. He was also one of those who'd been unable to keep up once Kyle had taken off.

Since he hadn't been close enough to the shooting for his hearing to be affected, the young man lowered his eyes and quickly stepped back so he was out of sight.

"They wanted to help, Mace," Hank said in a somewhat scolding manner. "And that's just what they would've done if they could. Lack of experience don't make them yellow."

Although he didn't appreciate being talked to like that, Mace nodded to concede the rancher's point. "Yeah. I guess you're right about that. As it was, those rustlers were the only ones to get themselves hurt."

"So that's who you think those men were?" Hank asked. "Rustlers?"

"That's my guess. What do you think, Kyle?"

"Makes sense, I guess."

Hank's eyes narrowed as he took a few seconds to study Kyle's face. "There something else you want to say?"

"Just that most rustlers are after as many head of cattle or horses they can get their hands on," Kyle said. "These men were waiting for us. Almost like they wanted to draw blood rather than just steal."

Taking that in, Hank took another sip of coffee. Behind him, the wind rattled a window against its frame. After looking over the faces in front of him, Hank's eyes came to rest upon one of those faces in particular. "So, Clint. It sounds like you were a big help out there."

"I was under fire just like everyone else and defended myself just like they did."

"Sounds to me like you did more than just hold your own. That is, unless Kyle was exaggerating."

The only response Clint gave was a shrug.

"How long have you been working here?" Hank asked.

Before answering that, Clint truly had to take a moment to think. "I guess it's been a few weeks."

"It'll be a month before too long," Hank added. Tapping his forehead, he said, "I've got a good memory for things like that. It's either that or deal with some mighty unhappy men come payday. I don't mean to pry, but I never really did get a chance to sit down and talk to you. All I remember about the day you got here was that your horse was in need of a few new shoes and you looked like you'd been raised by wolves."

Clint smirked at that, mostly because the rancher wasn't far from the truth. "You do have a good memory."

"So what brought you here?"

"Just what I told you before. Why do you ask?"

"Because my men almost got killed by a bunch of gunmen. By the sound of it, you're pretty handy with the iron yourself."

Clint nodded once, knowing that his actions had already done plenty of speaking for him.

"Just seems like a coincidence, is all."

"What does?" Clint asked. When he saw the hesitation on Hank's face, he added, "Go on. Say what's on your mind."

"We don't get a whole lot of gunhands around here. Not real ones, anyway." The rancher shifted in his seat as if suddenly the most comfortable chair in the room had become the least. "Now there's these killers picking fights with my men . . . and you right there among them. Among my men, I mean."

"Speaking of the other hands around here," Kyle said. "Most of them are pretty anxious to make themselves known and show their faces."

"I haven't been hiding," Clint pointed out.

"But you haven't been like the rest, either."

"Is that a problem?"

"Right about now, it looks like you might be hiding something," Kyle said.

From the other section of the group, Mace let out a snorting breath. "After what he did out there, I don't care how much Clint wants to keep to himself. Hell, I don't care if that's even his real name."

"You did a hell of a thing out there, Clint," Kyle said quickly. "I'm not trying to cast aspersions on you. All I'm saying is that it'd be good to know who's standing beside you when things go to hell like this."

Hank held out his hands as if he was breaking up a fight. "Nothing's gone to hell."

All three of the other men stopped and turned a hard look in the rancher's direction.

Blushing a bit under the suddenly close scrutiny, Hank said, "All right. Maybe it did slip a little."

Kyle shook his head and looked back to Clint. "Whatever it is, all I can tell you is what I think."

"And what's that?" Clint asked.

"That if you wanted to hurt us, you would have done just that when the lead started to fly. If you were in with those killers, it would have been a whole lot easier to wound one or two instead of kill one before he got to me."

"Could've just winged a horse or two," Mace pointed out.

"Or he could have steered us in another direction entirely," Kyle said in addition to his partner's comment. "The point is, we work together here just like President Lincoln said."

"Hang together or hang separately," Clint recited. "That's a hell of a choice to make."

"Yeah, but it's the one we got right now."

The truth of the matter was that several other choices sprung to Clint's mind at that point in time. Many of them involved other sources of help that might be of use to the folks at the Double Briar. Some of the choices involved what direction Clint would go if he just picked up and put the ranch behind him altogether.

But something else stuck in Clint's head. Actually, it stuck more in his craw than anywhere else. He didn't like being shot at. He also didn't like seeing good men get hurt at the whim of dangerous assholes with guns. And there was also someone else to consider. Clint wasn't Andy's best friend, but he knew the younger man didn't deserve to be forgotten.

"All right then," Clint said while looking around to the others seated in front of him. "What would make you feel better?"

"Well," Hank said, "you never did give me your last name."

"It's Adams. The name's Clint Adams."

It was a simple thing, but at least it was a start.

TEN

The bunkhouse at the Double Briar wasn't the first that Clint had ever slept in. It also wasn't the worst. Although the building was basically one long room separated into pieces by a few screens and the bunks themselves, they weren't bad accommodations.

Most bunkhouses weren't much better than sleeping on the ground. At least that way, a man had some room to stretch out and didn't need to worry about a dozen other neighbors waiting for him to fall asleep so they could help themselves to his belongings. The Double Briar had a different feel to it, and the men working there got along more like a family.

After what had happened that night, however, they were getting along more like an Army division.

A night watch had been set up and the men were sleeping in shifts. In the time that Clint, Kyle and Mace had had their conversation with Hank, word had spread throughout the ranch like wildfire. Most of the stories going around concerned the shoot-out. Others were about Andy, where he might be, if he was alive or dead, and who might be next to disappear.

Clint didn't have to hear the stories to know they were

going around. He could see what was on the other men's
minds just by looking at them as he walked by on his way to
his bunk. Those eyes were anxious and tired at the same
time. They were frightened and angry at what had happened.

They were soldiers' eyes. It was a shame to see them in
the faces of men who just wanted to work for a place to
stay and food in their bellies.

Of course, by the time he got to his bunk, Clint realized
that his own eyes had been affected as well. He had plenty
of things going through his head that made the night seem
a little more grim than it truly was. Once he realized that,
he took a deep breath and pressed his palms against his
brow.

Fatigue seeped into him like the cold winter air. And
when he looked up again, he saw the others in the bunkhouse a little clearer.

The men in there were frayed at the edges and a little
rattled. They all needed to take a moment for themselves
and let their hearts slow down to their normal pace. Once
that happened, they would be fine.

Sometimes, all it took was a quiet moment to sort things
out. Once he'd had one of those for himself, Clint realized
that he'd made the right decision before leaving Hank's
study a few minutes ago.

The front door to the bunkhouse swung open and a thin
figure stood in the doorway. Clint recognized who it was
right away. Considering that only men had walked into the
bunkhouse for the last couple of minutes, spotting a
woman's attractive shape wasn't all that hard.

She stepped inside, which was enough for some of the
light to touch her blond hair. Although a few of the men
raced to button their shirts or pat down their hair, most of
them merely looked up at the blonde and smiled. They
smiled even wider when they saw she was carrying a large
basket in one hand and holding a coffeepot in the other.

"There's still plenty of food if anyone wants it," she announced. "Since dinner was interrupted, I made sure that none of it was tossed out until everyone got some. I brought some sandwiches and coffee for those of you who were going out on watch."

"Bless yer soul, Percy," one of the men by the door said. "That smells awfully good."

Setting down the basket and coffee was akin to tossing food to a pack of dogs. In no time at all, it was split up and devoured. After that, plenty more headed out to find some more to fill their stomachs.

The blonde walked further into the bunkhouse and exchanged words with a few of the men along the way. She kept right on moving, however, until she got to the bunk toward the back of the building situated in a corner.

"Did you get a chance to eat anything?" she asked.

Clint was still perched on the edge of his bunk. "Just some coffee."

"That's not a proper meal."

"I wasn't too hungry at the time."

"Well, what about now?"

Clint looked at her and shrugged. His eyes then wandered over to the other men who were either making their way to the door or working on the sandwiches they'd managed to grab before the basket was emptied. "Seems like they don't know what to make of me."

"Who?" Percy asked. "These fellas or Hank?"

"Take your pick. Actually, now that I think about it all, I can't say that I blame any of them for being a little uncertain. I didn't really act like the warmest person to get along with."

Sitting down beside him on the bed, the blonde leaned in a little closer and said, "I think you're plenty warm. Especially after that first—"

Clint cut her off by gently placing his fingers upon her lips. Her mouth was soft and wisps of breath were still coming out from the last word she'd spoken. Even as she quieted herself, she let her voice turn into a sigh, which warmed plenty more than the tips of Clint's fingers.

"Mr. Ossutt didn't ask me too many questions when I got here, but he did lay down a few rules. One of them was to steer clear of the women around the place. He's just as protective of his daughter as he is of you, Percy."

"He means well," she whispered, sending even more of a tremor down Clint's spine. "I told you not to worry. It's not like you had to force yourself on me. And I told you I don't like it when you call me that."

"What? Percy? That's your name."

"That's what everyone calls me around here. I like it when you say my proper name."

"I know you do, Phoebe."

She smiled and closed her eyes a bit as if the sound of Clint's voice was rubbing along her naked back. When she opened her eyes again, she said, "Most of the cowboys around here said it wrong on purpose or otherwise, so I just let them call me Percy. Hank calls me that as a little joke. He's a good man, though. Treats me like one of his own."

"That's probably why he threatened to have anyone who touched you dragged out of here by their . . . Let's just say it wasn't anything I'd like to be tied to a horse."

Phoebe kept herself from laughing at the grimace on Clint's face and got up. Extending a hand and smiling, she said, "You still need to eat and get some rest after all that's happened. Come on, let's get you taken care of."

ELEVEN

Although most of the people walking from the bunkhouse were headed to where the food was being served, Clint and Phoebe split off into a different direction. As soon as they were out of plain sight, she reached back to grab his hand and pull him along anxiously behind the main house.

By the time they got to the narrow door underneath a small awning sticking out from the wall, they were both eager to get inside. Part of that was because of the biting cold in the air, which got worse with every passing minute. An even bigger part was because of the heat inside them, which was growing hotter twice as fast.

Phoebe used a key to open the small door and all but pushed Clint inside before stepping in herself. When she turned around after closing and locking the door again, Clint was waiting for her. He stepped up and pressed both hands flat against the door frame on either side of Phoebe's head.

They were standing in a hallway that was only long enough to accommodate the two of them. A few lanterns from the next room provided some light which trickled in past Clint's body and head. The last bit of illumination that brushed onto Phoebe's face showed the excited surprise she was feeling when Clint descended upon her.

For a moment, he lingered just in front of her. He waited there so he could feel the heat from her body through the clothes that kept their bare skin from touching. Unable to hold out more than a few seconds, Clint leaned in the rest of the way so he could plant a passionate kiss onto her lips.

Phoebe responded immediately. Leaning back against the door, she gave in to his every move while bringing her arms around his torso so her palms could slide up his back. She kept her hands moving on him, tracing the lines of his muscular shoulders before finding her way up over his neck and into his hair.

Clint's hands were busy as well. As their kiss became more and more intense, he felt up and down along her body, savoring the feel of her hips swaying back and forth in an intense rhythm. Soon, his palms grazed against the nape of her back and then glided down to cup her tight little backside.

"Oh God," Phoebe moaned as she twisted her head to one side and let out the breath she'd been holding. As soon as the words were out of her mouth, she pressed her lips against Clint's skin once more. This time, she nibbled along the side of his neck. Her breaths became harsh and louder as his hands squeezed her buttocks and almost lifted her off her feet.

After moving his hands up along the sides of her breasts for a moment, Clint reached back down so he could cup her once again. It seemed that Phoebe was thinking along the same lines as he was, because she immediately hopped up so he could lift her. From there, she wrapped her legs around Clint's waist and smiled broadly as she felt herself being carried away from the door and down the hall.

"And here I thought I'd fix you a nice supper," she said teasingly.

Clint smirked and nodded. "Sure. That's why you brought me back here rather than where the food is."

"I've got plenty of food for us."

"And it'll all taste even better after we've had a chance to work up an appetite."

Tightening her grip around him, Phoebe leaned down to place a few more kisses upon Clint's neck. "Sounds good to me."

Stopping at the foot of a small bed, Clint set Phoebe down on the edge of it and started unbuttoning his shirt.

Apart from the bed itself, there wasn't a whole lot else in the room. Despite the lack of fancy furniture, the room seemed plenty comfortable. There was a rug, which covered most of the floor, and thick cotton curtains over the window. There was a narrow wardrobe in one corner and a small table in another. Placed here and there were various bits and pieces to reflect the person who lived there. Like most of the men on Ossutt's payroll, Phoebe worked at the Double Briar but she was obviously cared for like a family member.

For the moment, the only thing that Clint concerned himself with was the bed in the middle of the room and the small fireplace on the adjacent wall. The fireplace was only wide enough to hold a few split logs, but was enough to give the room some heat. It was also enough to throw a flickering light upon Phoebe's smooth, bare shoulders as she pulled open the front of her blouse and peeled it off completely.

TWELVE

She tossed the clothing to one side without taking her eyes off of Clint. Watching as he kicked off his boots and began taking down his pants, she eagerly reached out with both hands to help him with the task.

"Here," she whispered. "Let me."

With that, she pulled his pants down and ran her hands along the sides of his legs. Phoebe kept one hand moving up over his stomach as she slipped the other between his legs. She cupped him gently and brushed her lips against his growing erection. As her eyes moved up, she got a look at his face as she opened her mouth and slipped the tip of his penis over her waiting tongue.

Now it was Clint's turn to let out a slow, measured breath. He reached down to slide his fingers through her hair while savoring the feel of her mouth closing around his cock. When she began bobbing her head back and forth, Clint guided her pace with his hands.

Phoebe moaned slightly at the feel of his insistent hands. She could feel him growing harder in her mouth, which made her own breaths come even quicker. After taking him all the way into her mouth, she began swirling her tongue around him in a slow circle. Although she knew

46

Clint was loving every second, she still felt his hands gently easing her away from him.

When she looked up at him, Phoebe put on an expression that was more sexy than disappointed. "What's the matter?" she asked, even though she knew perfectly well what the answer was. "Didn't you like that?"

Clint started to speak, but knew he didn't really need to say a word. Instead, he reached down and pulled her back to her feet. He then lifted her up and set her down onto the bed.

The moment she felt the mattress beneath her, Phoebe lay back and opened her legs to allow Clint to climb on top of her. As he did so, Clint pulled Phoebe's skirt down over her hips until she was able to kick it onto the floor.

Now they were both naked, their bodies pressed together in a way that they'd both been wanting for what now felt like an eternity. Clint savored the moment by moving his hands up and down along her sides, feeling the smooth flesh beneath his palms as if it was for the very first time.

Phoebe arched her back and stretched like a contented cat. She almost let out something akin to a purr as Clint's hands slid over every one of her curves before settling upon the soft mounds of her breasts. All it took was a few gentle brushes from his thumbs and forefingers to get her nipples fully erect. When he continued to tease her nipples with those same fingers, Phoebe let out a giggling squeal.

"You know just what to do to me, Clint."

"Practice makes perfect."

"You haven't been here that long."

"I know," he replied. "So just think how much better it can get the longer I stay."

With her eyes closed, Phoebe rested her head against her pillow so she could fully savor Clint's caress. She sighed contentedly once his weight came down on top of her and then opened her legs a bit more to let him settle between them.

Clint reached down and guided himself to the soft,

moist spot that waited for him. The downy hair between her legs was the same color as the hair on her head, making it seem even more like spun silk. He slid inside of her easily, and she accepted every inch of his penis with another one of her soft, purring moans.

"That feels so good," she whispered.

But Clint didn't say a word. Instead, he propped himself up a bit with one arm as he began pumping his hips slowly forward and back. His other arm slipped underneath Phoebe's shoulders so he could hold her as he moved in and out of her.

This wasn't the first time they'd been naked and in each other's arms. That familiarity showed in the way they moved to adjust themselves slightly at just the right times to please each other. Without needing to say a word, Phoebe got Clint to roll onto his back so she could climb on top of him.

Her soft, yet muscular body writhed on top of his as she rubbed against his bare flesh. Soon, she felt his hands upon her once more, working their way over her sides and then up along her back. Phoebe leaned her head back as a wide smile shone across her face.

After a few subtle shifts, the tip of Clint's penis was slipping inside of her again. Phoebe pressed her hands flat against his chest and lowered herself down until she was fully enveloping him. As the last bit of his length was pushed into her, Phoebe's eyes snapped open and a pleasurable moan escaped her lips.

Clint smiled as he watched her. He placed his hands upon her hips and started grinding slowly beneath her body. Soon, Phoebe was rocking back and forth on top of him, riding his cock while slowly tossing her hair from side to side.

The bed creaked beneath them louder and louder. When the narrow headboard started tapping against the wall, Phoebe froze like she'd been caught with a stolen horse.

"You think anyone's heard us?" she asked.

"If they haven't heard by now, they're either deaf or don't give a damn."

Giving him a smile that was part amused and part annoyed, Phoebe smacked Clint's bare chest with the flat of her hand. "Remember what we were saying about Hank? He might get a little upset if he knew what was going on in here. Why do you think I need to sneak you in the back?"

Clint reached up with one hand so he could pull Phoebe's face down close to his own. "Then maybe we should stop talking," he said before silencing her with a firm kiss on the lips.

All of Phoebe's protests melted away in the same way that her body melted against Clint's. Soon, she was riding him vigorously again. Thanks to Clint's repeated efforts, the thought of keeping quiet flew further and further from her mind.

THIRTEEN

Although the sky outside Phoebe's window was still black as pitch, dawn was close enough to feel like it was breathing down the back of Clint's neck. He and Phoebe were still in her room, wearing nothing but the barest of essentials under several layers of thick quilts and blankets. A fire crackled in the little fireplace across the room, which still wasn't enough to keep away the encroaching winter chill.

Plates and utensils were piled in heaps on both sides of the bed. The food that Phoebe had brought back in between their lovemaking sessions was nothing but a fond memory. Clint sat with his back propped against the headboard and Phoebe curled up beside him with her head on his chest. Her hand wandered over his stomach beneath the covers.

She moved away from him and slipped out from under the covers so she could collect some clothing and head out the door. Considering that she was in charge of keeping up the main house, it was nothing to have her slip in and out of the room several times when he'd spend the night. Clint only had to wait a few minutes for her to come back in again and shut the door quietly.

"Has there been any word about Andy?" Clint asked.

He could see her shaking her head. "Not yet."

Clint swung his feet over the side of the bed and started picking up his clothes so he could pull them on. In the time he'd been staying at the Double Briar, he'd gotten used to getting in and out of Phoebe's room making less noise than a cat on hardwood floors.

"And I'll be riding out at first light," he said. "If Andy hasn't come back by that time, he definitely is in some trouble."

"You don't sound too hopeful about finding him."

Clint looked over to make sure that Phoebe wasn't really looking for comfort rather than his honest opinion. "I'm counting on finding him," he told her. "I'm just afraid he won't be in the condition that everyone's hoping for."

"You think he's hurt? Or . . . worse?"

"All I know for certain is that if he fell from his horse, he wouldn't have been so hard to find. He could have hollered for help, shot his gun in the air, or anything else to draw some attention. For that matter, where the hell is his horse? Even a spooked animal will be more likely to head back home before too long rather than just pick a direction and start running."

"Did you tell any of this to Hank?"

"I don't have to. Any man who's worth his salt on a ranch would know this much without being told. Finding Andy might just make things a little clearer as far as our other set of visitors is concerned."

"You mean the rustlers?"

"Whoever they are."

Phoebe was all but fully dressed by now. The laces that cinched up the front of her blouse were tied, but not tightly enough to cover the cotton undershirt which was more for warmth than appearances. Her rumpled skirt dropped down to cover the boots that came up well past her ankles. If not for the worried expression on her face, she would have been downright sexy.

"You don't think they're rustlers?" she asked.

Clint had his eyes on her as he stood up and reached for the gunbelt draped over one of her chairs. Doing his best to casually buckle on the Colt, he said, "Hank and Kyle were right about one thing. Rustlers come after cows. They don't stand around waiting for a fight."

"Then what are they? Killers? Are they after everyone here at the ranch?"

The more Phoebe spoke, the deeper the concern in her voice became. Clint stepped forward and brushed his hand along the side of her face. Just by doing that simple thing, he could feel the tension in her start to ease up. Inside, he was regretting saying out loud what he was thinking rather than keep the thoughts to himself.

"I'm sure these aren't the first armed men that have started trouble around here," Clint said.

"No, they're not."

"Things just seem worse because all of the men aren't accounted for yet. Once we find Andy, we can piece together what's going on. Things aren't usually half as bad as they seem at first."

"Well, by the looks of things, they seem pretty bad."

Clint's hand was on the grip of his holstered Colt, and he noticed that Phoebe's eyes had drifted in that direction when she said those last words. "What do you mean?"

"I went out to check on how everything was going. You know, with the watch and all."

"Yeah."

"They never did find Andy," she said.

"That's really not too big of a surprise. It's dark enough out there that a man might have a hard time finding his own feet unless he was crouching down. And if he was hurt, Andy probably just crawled in under his blanket and passed out for the night. He could have even built a small fire and it would have been easy to miss. Ossutt owns a hell of a lot of land, you know."

"I know," Phoebe said with a subtle nod. "But everyone's heading out with guns and a look in their eyes like they mean to use them."

"I'm sure Hank doesn't want to get his men killed."

"He was one of the ones carrying guns, Clint. Him and Kyle. They were out all night."

Clint made a fist and knocked it against the closest thing he could find. The wardrobe was the unlucky piece of furniture, and it rattled against the force of Clint's frustrated blow.

"Dammit," Clint snarled. "They said they were going to wait until first light. I talked to Kyle and Hank last night and specifically asked to be out there with them when they headed out in the morning." Turning to look directly at Phoebe once again, he asked, "How long ago did they head out? Do you know where they went?"

"It must have been some time after I got our dinner. I heard Hank and Kyle talking when I went to the kitchen and back."

"And you don't know where they went?"

She shook her head. "But you can still have a word with them. They were just getting ready to head out again a few minutes ago."

"They're here?"

She nodded.

Clint was out the door before he'd gotten his hat pulled down all the way onto his head.

FOURTEEN

When Clint stomped down the main hall of the house, he could see the first rays of dawn glinting in through the eastern windows. The first floor was laid out in an open manner with only a few large rooms behind wide doorways. The smell of bread cooking and coffee brewing caught his attention, but wasn't enough to pull him away from the task at hand.

He made it nearly to the front of the house before spotting the two men he was after. Hank Ossutt and Kyle stood holding steaming cups in their hands. Both of them turned quickly toward Clint as he approached. Kyle's hand reflexively twitched in the direction of his holster before he recognized Clint's face.

"When you said you'd meet us at first light, you weren't kidding," Hank said with a chuckle.

"Did you two head out without me last night?" Clint asked.

Hank's expression had been weary as well as a little amused at Clint's entrance. Now a hint of anger crept into his features. "I don't believe I need to check with you about anything I do on my own land, Adams."

"I didn't mean it like that," Clint said, doing his best to

take the edge from his voice. "After what happened last night, I thought you'd know better than to go out in the dark where there could be another ambush waiting for you."

Hank's eyes remained focused on Clint. For a few seconds, he didn't say a word. Instead, he took that time to take a breath and let it out in a haggard rush.

Standing at Hank's side, Kyle was no longer reaching for his gun. The move had been a reflex and now his hand was reaching out to pat Hank on the shoulder. "We could use his help, you know. With a man like Clint Adams on our side, even killers like these might think twice."

Hank nodded toward Kyle and then looked back to Clint. His rugged face was weary and seemed to have aged ten years since the previous night. "You're right, Clint," he finally said. "I did say that I'd wait for you. Maybe heading out on our own wasn't such a good idea."

When Kyle glanced over at Clint, there was a look in his eyes that had "He won't listen to me" written all over it.

"But I don't like the thought of leaving a man out there in the cold," Hank continued. "Especially since he might be hurt."

Lowering his voice, Clint said, "And he might be dead."

The words were like blades that cut right to the quick. Although he didn't like to be so blunt when talking about someone's friend, Clint could see that his point was made real well and real quick.

"We might not know much about who those men are out there," Clint said, "but we do know they're ready and willing to pull their triggers. I know something about men like that. I also know a bit about how to deal with them. I'm offering my help to you, Hank. You want it or not?"

"Of course I do."

"Then do me a favor and don't go rushing headfirst into the breach before you really know what you're getting into."

Some more of the anger in Hank's eyes faded. It was replaced by a weary smile. "I haven't answered to anyone for
a long time, Adams, and I don't intend on starting now. But
I will admit I'm a rancher and not a lawman or gunhand."

Hank paused slightly before saying that last word,
which was enough to let Clint know that he didn't mean
any disrespect in using the term.

"So I'll keep you in the know about any more moves I
want to make, no matter how thick-headed they may be."

"All right," Clint said. "But at least listen to my advice
and give me a chance to pitch in before you make a thick-
headed mistake. Agreed?"

Hank nodded and slapped Clint on the shoulder in the
same way he'd done with Kyle and Mace the night before.
"You got a deal. Now grab some coffee and whatever food
you can carry because we're riding out in ten minutes. The
horses are being brought around front, so you'd best be
there with your coat on. It's a hell of a cold day out there."

With that, Hank chucked Kyle on the shoulder and
stomped off to another part of the house. Kyle remained
with Clint in the hall.

"Why are you messing with all of this?" Kyle asked.
"You don't have anything at stake here. Hell, plenty of the
hands that have worked here longer than you have cut and
run in the last few hours. Why aren't you one of them?"

"Because you're good folks," Clint replied. "And I can
help you."

Smirking, Kyle said, "That's not much of a reason."

"From where I stand, those are some of the best reasons
there are."

FIFTEEN

Although Clint thought the owner of the Double Briar Ranch might have been a little unwise in his decisions the night before, it was obvious that Hank Ossutt had a good handle on the weather. The moment Clint stepped outside of the house, the breath was stolen from his lungs by a rough breeze that sliced through him like frozen steel.

Eclipse had seen his fair share of harsh weather, but even the Darley Arabian needed some time to adjust to the brutal cold. After riding for a quarter mile or so, the stallion's muscles loosened up and his steps became more fluid as he carried Clint out onto the rancher's land.

The three riders formed a wedge pattern with Hank in the lead and Clint and Kyle slightly behind and to either side. Together, they rode in a trail that started at the house and spiraled outward from there.

The sun had broken over the horizon and was now hanging low in the sky. Clint always felt like he could see better and hear more in the winter. Times like these, however, made him realize that the chill in the air was probably just doing a hell of a job of sharpening his senses. That rang true even more as he recalled a sheriff's deputy saying that he would rather get shot in the summer than in the winter.

"Everything hurts more in the cold," the deputy had said.

Clint hoped that he wouldn't have to test that theory out for himself anytime in the near future.

Although they'd kept their eyes and ears open through-out the entire ride, all three men paid extra close attention as they found themselves in the section of land where Kyle and Andy had last parted ways. Plenty of others had looked in this area before them, but that didn't stop them from tak-ing another pass for themselves.

Kyle broke off from the other two and moved to a spot where he could look out toward the fence line. "This is where we were, Hank," Kyle explained. "I told Andy to meet me back here."

"And that was the last time you saw him?" Hank asked.

"Yes, sir."

"Which way did he ride off to?"

Kyle pointed in the direction Andy had gone, and Clint looked in that direction himself. Despite the brighter light in the sky, it didn't look much different from the last time he'd been there.

"Then that's the way we're going." Acknowledging Clint with a nod, Hank added, "All of us."

"As long as we're here," Clint said, "we can make our way back to the spot where the shooting happened. Maybe we'll spot something now that we couldn't in the dark."

"Let's do it." With that, Hank snapped his reins and got his horse moving.

Eclipse was only too eager to follow since that meant getting the heat flowing through his muscles once again. Kyle rode right beside Clint.

For the first forty or fifty yards, Clint was hopeful.

That hope began to falter during the twenty or so yards following those. Apart from the fact that nobody was seeing much of anything at all, the winds were beating the grass back and forth like it was a punishment. There was a layer of frost on the ground, but it already looked as if it had been churned by a passing train.

These factors alone meant that tracks would be next to impossible to spot from horseback. Climbing down from the saddle to get a closer look was the start of a mighty big job unless someone could find a suitable place to start.

"What about the land over that way?" Clint asked, pointing in the direction of the house and beyond.

Without having to look, Hank replied, "That's where the rest of the stables and barns are. There are some head of cattle over there, but not many. Just the ones that weren't healthy or old enough to make the last drive."

"Then we might as well stop here and get a look," Clint said. "Maybe we can pick up a trace of him that'll show us where to go next."

Kyle brought his horse to a stop after another couple feet. "Sounds good. At least we might be able to sit still long enough to hear him hollering for us or get a hint of where he spent the night."

Shrugging, Hank didn't seem too enthused by the prospects the other two were describing. But since it was better than nothing, he shrugged and swung down from his saddle.

A shot cracked in the distance, followed by the hiss of lead speeding through the air.

Clint ducked low and had his Colt in hand in the blink of an eye.

Kyle took a little more time to draw his gun, but not much.

Hank still had one foot in the stirrups as he tried to drop down and get out of the line of fire. His ankle twisted in the leather and he just barely managed to catch himself with his quickly outstretched hands. He dangled from the stirrup like a fish on a hook while clenching his teeth so hard that they could almost be heard grinding together.

All the while, the rancher was pulling his foot against the stirrup. Finally, he twisted the right way and his ankle popped out from where it was being held. Of course, that also caused the rest of him to drop down awkwardly, and it was all Hank could do to land roughly on his backside.

"Son of a bitch," the rancher snarled through gritted teeth.

"You all right, Hank?" Clint asked. "Are you hit?"

"No," Hank grunted. "But that damn bullet didn't miss by much."

"It came from over that way," Kyle shouted.

Clint looked to where Kyle was pointing and saw the telltale wisp of smoke rising in the distance. If not for the open range and the stark clarity of the morning air, none of them might have been able to spot the only sign showing where the shot had come from.

Putting together what he could see with what he'd heard, Clint figured that the bullet might not have missed at all if Hank had stayed in his saddle for another second.

"All right, you bastards," Hank growled as he struggled to flop over and get his feet under him. "Let's see what yer made of."

Before Clint could stop him, Hank was straightening up and lurching forward. The rancher didn't make it one whole step, however, before he winced and twisted downward as though an invisible hand had violently grabbed him by the collar.

Another shot cracked through the air, coming from a spot fairly close to the one Kyle had just pointed out. Clint spotted the smoke, which looked like a bit of cloud being spit out from the ground. Even as the sound of the shot was just making it to his ears, Clint had taken quick aim and squeezed his trigger.

Lead hissed through the air, traveling in both directions. Clint's was around waist level and the incoming bullet was on a slightly higher path.

Clint knew better than to think he could hit the other man, especially since he couldn't really see who was doing the shooting. He'd only hoped to give the hidden sharpshooter something to worry about. Since the incoming fire had held off for a bit, Clint guessed that he'd been successful.

"We've got to get out of the open," Clint hollered to Kyle and Hank.

Kyle's only response was a quick, puzzled look thrown in Clint's direction.

Surveying his surroundings with a few quick glances of his own, Clint realized what had put that look on Kyle's face.

The spot where they were was in the middle of a stretch of flat prairie that spread out for acres in each direction.

There was nowhere else to go.

SIXTEEN

Clint had seen this situation more than once. He'd tried to be on the other end of it most of the time, but there wasn't much he could do about it now. Any way he thought about it, being ambushed in the middle of a prairie without catching sight of his attackers was a short path into a brick wall.

For that reason, Clint decided to stop thinking about the situation and just do his damndest to live through it.

One thing he knew for certain was that sitting in their current spot was a death sentence. All a man needed was to know which end of a rifle to point in their direction and he'd be able to pick off Clint and the two others with just a little help from a friend or two. Certain that there had to be more than one out there, Clint didn't even bother trying to spot them.

He also didn't bother trying to say much of anything to Hank or Kyle. It looked as though Hank was nursing a twisted ankle, and Kyle was doing his best to keep from getting his own head blown off as more shots started coming in from other directions.

Hustling over to Hank's side, Clint reached down and helped the rancher get upright. "How bad is it?" Clint asked.

"It ain't broken, but it hurts like a bastard," Hank replied.

"Give me your gun."

"What?"

"You need to get onto your horse and back to the house. You'll only be firing wildly during that, so give me your gun. I'll put it to better use."

All it took was one look into Clint's eyes for the rancher to be convinced. He handed over his pistol. "Take it. I'll get onto that horse on my own or not at all."

There wasn't enough time for more than that as Clint took the rancher's gun with his left hand. He then rushed over to Eclipse and jumped into the saddle using nothing more than a toe in the stirrup and one arm crooked around the saddle horn.

The Darley Arabian shifted beneath him, proving just how much of a team he and Clint truly were.

Clint touched his heels to the horse's sides just enough to get Eclipse moving. From there, it was a matter of balance and willpower that kept him upright in the saddle as the stallion built up to a charge into the line of fire.

Despite the fact that he was running headfirst into a hornet's nest, Clint felt better about the situation already. Eclipse was accounted for, Hank was on his way back, and Kyle appeared to be doing just fine on his own. Once he started firing a pistol from each hand, Clint's mood improved even more.

He didn't have any targets at first. Clint's only concern was driving back whoever it was that had sprung the ambush. Thanks to the fact that Eclipse was calmer under fire than most men, Clint got close enough to spot one of the other gunmen in a matter of seconds.

It wasn't much more than a glimpse of movement from the corner of his eye, but that was enough to catch Clint's attention. From his higher vantage point on the stallion's back, the flat prairie was now working in Clint's favor.

A man dressed in battered leathers and a brown coat had been laying with his belly against the earth. He'd stayed put as Clint started firing in his general direction, but the thunder of Eclipse's approaching hooves was more than enough to flush him from his spot.

The man rolled away from the oncoming horse and rider, letting out a curse that was lost amid the roar of gunfire and charging stallion. Clint picked up on the motion to his left and shifted in the saddle just as the man of the ground was bringing a rifle around to bear.

Clint's modified Colt swung across his body while he took aim with the gun he'd taken from Hank. Both pistols went off, the Colt just ahead of the second firearm, sending two rounds through the other man's chest which practically nailed him to the ground.

The moment Clint saw that he'd taken care of one gunman, he started looking for the next one. He didn't know exactly how many were out there, but he was certain there was more than one. As if to confirm his thought right then and there, another shot cracked through the air and hissed by his head.

Clint shifted in his saddle and sent a pair of bullets toward the sound of the shot. He also laid down a curtain of lead which covered a wide arc in front of Eclipse's path. That seemed to silence the shooting for the moment, so Clint brought the Darley Arabian to a stop.

Glancing over his shoulder, Clint saw that Hank had managed to get onto his horse and was riding off. Kyle was mounted up as well, but headed toward Clint rather than the direction of the house. Clint quickly looked around while he stuffed Hank's pistol under his belt and reloaded the Colt.

His ears were still ringing from the shooting, and thunder was still rolling through the air. Even with all of that, Clint was struck by how quiet it had gotten in such a short amount of time. Apart from the echoes of the fight, there wasn't much else that could be heard over the rustle of wind.

Suddenly, a sound made it to Clint's ears that might not have even caught his attention at any other time. It wasn't much more than a ripple in the air, but at that moment it seemed like glass shattering on a quiet day. Clint recognized the sound as leather against leather followed by the grunt of a horse.

With the land being so flat, Clint knew that the horse couldn't be too close to him. That only left a little stand of trees just up ahead. Sure enough, that was where he spotted a sudden burst of motion once he got Eclipse headed in that direction.

A tan horse burst from those trees like a quail that had been flushed by a hunting dog. It charged out and immediately steered away from Clint so it could thunder off toward the fence line.

"Oh no you don't," Clint said under his breath as he snapped the reins.

Eclipse responded with a few huffing breaths and was soon charging off in pursuit.

SEVENTEEN

Clint couldn't help but smile as he was carried toward that gunman as if he'd been strapped to the back of a cannonball. Eclipse pounded over the frozen grasslands with steam pouring from both nostrils. The stallion's breath came in mighty heaves as his head churned forward intently.

He'd taken off practically at the same time as the last fresh round had been slipped into the Colt's cylinder. Clint snapped the gun shut with a flick of his wrist and then stretched his arm out ahead of him to take careful aim.

It didn't take long for his own body to move in time to Eclipse's gait, and once that was accomplished, Clint's hand was steadied considerably. He pulled in a breath, let it out and squeezed the trigger. Although Eclipse twitched a bit at the shot going off over his head, the Darley Arabian was plenty used to that noise and didn't miss a step.

The shot from the Colt was a little high and to the right. The only reason for that, however, was because that was exactly where Clint had wanted the bullet to go.

The rider ahead of him had been steering toward the right, obviously headed for something in that direction. For the moment, Clint's only priority was to keep that rider from getting to wherever he wanted to go.

He could hear gunshots behind him, so he figured that Kyle had found another gunman. Clint decided to let Kyle handle whatever he'd found, since it didn't sound like more than a few scattered shots. He set his sights, picked another target and squeezed off another shot.

The Colt barked one more time, sending a bullet right through the spot where the other rider had been headed. This time, the bullet got a little closer to drawing blood, which made the rider even more hesitant to make his turn.

Now that his route had been cut off for the moment, the rider looked around for another way to go, while hefting his rifle so he could take a shot at Clint. All of this didn't take more than a second or two, but that was plenty of time for Clint to draw up closer and come around to the rider's left.

Clint snapped Eclipse's reins and hunkered down in anticipation of the stallion's reply. Like clockwork, the Darley Arabian poured some more steam into his stride and got even closer to the other horse.

The gunman aimed roughly over his shoulder and pulled his trigger. His rifle was dangling from his grip and lurched even lower when the gunman took a quick turn to one side. Although the shot didn't come close to hitting Clint, it punched a hole in the dirt a yard or so short of Eclipse's front legs.

Eclipse gave a subtle hop so he could jump over what felt like a rumble in the ground in front of him. Other than that, however, the stallion was practically unaffected.

Clint was close enough to place a shot anywhere he chose on the gunman without the slightest worry of coming up short. With the gunman looking over his shoulder on the side where all the shots had come from, that even forced the man to put his back to Clint.

Rather than take the easy shot, Clint waited another second so he could draw up even closer. The gunman's horse was doing well under the circumstances, but was no match to Eclipse's speed.

When he was right where he wanted to be, Clint let out a holler as though he was giving a hurried command to his horse. Although Eclipse didn't respond to the noise, the gunman sure did.

Twisting around in his saddle, the gunman was wearing a vicious smirk. He'd swung the rife completely around so he could take aim and shoot a pursuer who, he thought, had just tipped his hand at the wrong time. Rather than find a man struggling to control his horse, he found Clint to be twice as close as he'd expected.

Not only was Clint close enough to see the whites of the gunman's eyes, but he was close enough to reach out and grab hold of the man's rifle before it was anywhere close to aimed at him.

Clint's hand wrapped around the end of the barrel and closed tight. The only thing that saved him from getting burned right away was the fact that the air was cold enough to cool the steel and his hands were already cold as ice to begin with.

Once he had a grip on the rifle, Clint yanked it from the gunman's hands and pulled it back over his own shoulder. From there, he brought the rifle back along the same arc until it smacked solidly against the gunman's head.

The gunman let out a pained grunt and wobbled in his saddle. He lasted all of two seconds before dropping off the horse completely and landing in a heap upon the ground.

Clint brought Eclipse to a stop and circled back around to where the man had fallen. Along the way, he looked for any sign of other would-be ambushers lurking about.

"Looks like it's just you and me," Clint said as he approached the fallen gunman.

The man on the ground looked anything but pleased.

EIGHTEEN

It was tough to say how badly the gunman was hurt, but it was plain enough to see that he wasn't in the best of shape. Plenty of folks had died from a fall off their horse, and being dropped by a knock to the head offered plenty more painful opportunities.

As was the case for most assholes, however, this one made it through his fall and was able to cuss loudly about it.

"Son of a bitch!" the gunman shouted as he squirmed and shifted on the ground.

Eclipse came to a stop and scraped his front hooves against the ground, as if to remind the gunman that he'd almost shot the horse a few minutes ago. Another set of feet crunched against the soil—Clint's as he climbed down from the saddle and started walking over to the other man.

Clint took two steps and ended his third by stepping down upon the man's wrist. He didn't exert much pressure; just enough to keep him in place while Clint plucked the gun from a holster strapped around the other man's waist.

"There," Clint said. "Now we can talk."

"Talk, my ass!"

"That didn't make a whole lot of sense, but it looks like you're in a bit of pain."

"Fuck you!"

Clint smirked at the way something as simple as the tone in his voice could push someone else to their limit. It was an old trick used at the poker tables and came in just as handy now.

Keeping the smirk on his face, Clint left his boot pressed against the man's wrist. In fact, he leaned on that foot even harder as he knelt down to get a little closer. "Then again, it's kind of hard for me to feel sorry for you since you and your buddies have been shooting at me for two days."

The other man had plenty of obscenities on the tip of his tongue, but decided to keep them there for the moment.

"Now you're getting quiet?" Clint asked. "That's a shame. I was hoping you'd be in the mood to talk." Fixing his eyes on the gunman, Clint put an edge in his stare that was enough to make the gunman wish he was in another part of the country. "Let's start out with who the hell you are."

The gunman didn't say a word. He did squirm a bit, however, when Clint twisted his foot against his trapped wrist.

"I see your leg's twisted up underneath you," Clint pointed out. "Maybe I should take a closer look at it."

Clint had never been the type of man to torture anyone and he wasn't about to start now. Of course, there was no way for the gunman to know that and nothing at all on Clint's face to show his true intentions.

"We're not after you," the gunman blurted out.

"That's a start. Go on." After pausing for a moment, all Clint had to do was move his foot enough for the gunman to feel it in order to get the other man's tongue loosened up again.

"Why don't you ask your boss?" the gunman spouted.

"If he didn't tell you anything about why we're here, then he ain't telling you much of anything. He's the one putting you in danger, not us."

"First of all," Clint said, "he's not the one that's been doing all the shooting. And second, you're the one that looks to be in the most danger right now."

"You just keep talking," the gunman said with a grin that showed bloodstained teeth. "I know you're the one that killed one of our boys last night. You'll pay for that, asshole. If'n you don't let me go right here and now, you'll pay even more. You and all them women you keep in that fancy house."

Clint's eyes narrowed as he stared down at the gunman. Although he could easily spot the bluster in the other man's words, he knew that there was some truth to them as well. Mostly, he was wasting time by staying put. Any longer in the open after all that shooting, and Clint would catch some lead himself.

"That's right," the gunman sneered, doing a good job of reading faces himself. "Keep on talking and you'll meet my friends. You'll get a real good look at 'em and then you can meet the devil, because that's where they'll send you."

"You know something? I think you might just have a point," Clint said.

The victorious smile on the gunman's face was short-lived. Before he could get too comfortable, he felt a dull pain thump into the sore spot on the side of his head. From there, it was a quick drop into blackness.

NINETEEN

Hank was getting anxious.

Although he'd fully intended on going back to the house, those plans changed once he'd made it up onto his horse and put some distance between himself and the shooting. He was an injured man, but he wasn't a cowardly one.

All it took was a strong breath to send shards of pain lancing through his twisted leg. As far as he could tell, that leg wasn't broken, but it wasn't exactly proper. But even if it was broke, it would have taken a hell of a lot more than that for him to leave his men out in the open and under fire. Reaching around to the back of his saddle, Hank's hand fell upon the very thing he'd been looking for: a sawed-off shotgun under a rolled up blanket.

Mostly, the shotgun had been used to break up fights, blast the occasional snake or spook a group of errant cows. Even though two out of three of those things required shooting into the air, Hank still felt competent enough to turn back and lend a hand to his men. That is, if they still needed it.

He knew better than to charge in when nerves were stretched to their limits, so he'd hung back and waited for a sign that he was needed. So far, the shooting had stopped and only the occasional voice or horse could be heard.

With the cold air swirling around him, Hank felt the winter's chill seep right down to the marrow in his bones. The longer he waited, the colder he felt. Most of that was now coming from the dread that he might have waited too long.

Taking a firm grip on the reins, Hank gave them a snap and held his shotgun at the ready. Just as he was going to get his horse moving even faster, he spotted a pair of riders coming together in the distance and heading straight for him.

There was a subtle rise in the land between him and those other riders, so Hank slowed down to make sure that he wasn't as exposed as the other two, who were now cresting that slope. The rancher's heart thumped against his ribs, speeding up with each passing second. Although he didn't know everything about guns, he knew his land well enough to be fairly certain he was out of most pistols' ranges.

If one of those riders was a marksman with a rifle, on the other hand, Hank was in a bit of trouble. But it was too late to worry about that now. He'd made his decision and was prepared to back it. Before too much longer, the other riders were close enough for him to realize that he didn't have anything to worry about after all.

Letting out the breath he'd been holding, Hank rode up to meet the two men. "I was starting to worry about you two."

Clint and Kyle were riding side by side, with Kyle moving just ahead. Neither of them looked like he was about to stop as they drew closer to where the rancher was waiting.

"You were supposed to get back to the house," Kyle said.

Hank watched as Kyle rode by him. "I couldn't just

leave you men out here like that. Even if I ain't much use, I can do something to help."

Clint was the next to ride by the rancher. "You want to help? You can start by lowering that shotgun."

Smirking, Hank quickly lowered the gun, which he'd almost forgotten was still aimed at both men. "Yeah. I thought you might need some cover in case those . . . What the hell?"

Hank's voice took an upward turn once he spotted the bundle strapped across Eclipse's back.

Situated behind Clint, the wounded gunman was tied down like a bedroll. Both arms were roped behind his back and his legs were lashed together as well. His head lolled from side to side as Eclipse's haunches shifted beneath it.

Hank stared at the limp body and asked, "Is he . . . ?"

"No," Kyle replied. "He's not dead, but that's not my idea."

"We're taking this one back to the house," Clint said. "He's still got plenty to tell us."

"I don't know if he'll be apt to talk," Hank said.

"I didn't say if he'd be apt to talk, willing to talk or wanting to talk. I said he had some more to tell us and he'll do just that."

The rancher flicked his reins so he could fall into step with the other two men as they made their way back to the house. Although Clint and Kyle were moving at a steady pace, they weren't going nearly as fast as they had on their way out.

Hank looked back and forth between Clint and the bundle he was carrying. "I know that these men have done wrong, but I can't say I like the idea of stringing them up or . . . however you meant to make him talk."

"Don't worry about that," Clint assured him. "I'm not stringing anyone up. Things may get a little noisy and we might have to rig up some sort of cell, but they're not getting bloody. In fact, I was hoping you had someone skilled enough to take a good look at his legs. He hurt at least one of them falling from his horse."

Studying the dried blood on the unconscious gunman's scalp, Hank asked, "You're telling me he fell?"

"Sure," Clint replied with a nod. "I cracked him on the head and he fell. I may not be ready to beat anything out of this man, but I wasn't about to let him shoot me, either. Does that sit well enough with you?"

Hank was shaking his head, more out of wonder than anything close to disapproval. "That sits with me just fine. I'm just surprised we caught such a big fish on our first time stepping up to the creek. I'm just glad to hear you don't intend on doing anything . . . gruesome."

Clint shook his head. "That's not the smart way to go about things anyway. We play our cards right and we'll have this one eating out of the palms of our hands without him knowing any better."

Laughing to himself, Hank's face dropped a little. He leaned in and whispered, "You sure he can't hear us right now?"

"If he was tough enough to hang in there after what he's been through and keep his wits enough to pay attention to every word we're saying, he wouldn't be strapped over the back of my horse right now."

That seemed to put the smile back onto Hank's face. "I don't know what you've got in mind, but I sure as hell want to watch what happens."

"Yeah," Clint replied with a little less enthusiasm. "Me, too."

TWENTY

Less than an hour after Clint, Hank and Kyle returned to the main cluster of buildings at the middle of the Double Briar Ranch, everyone on the property was up and busy. Breakfast was served in a quick, quiet manner. Where the dining hall was normally alive with casual chatter, it was now buzzing with whispered rumors and nervous speculation.

Everyone knew about what had happened and most of them had even gotten a look at the prisoner that had been brought back and stored in one of the smokehouses. And that wasn't the only man to capture a good portion of the conversation. Word about The Gunsmith being in their midst was spreading just as quickly.

Clint heard some of those whispers as he walked by. If he had any doubts that he was the subject of their talk, they were squelched when the whispers picked up the moment he walked past. It was mostly for that reason that he'd done his best to keep a low profile upon getting to the ranch.

On one hand, Clint wanted to get away from the shadow of The Gunsmith, which followed him wherever he went. That shadow was made up of plenty of rumors and even some outright lies. The shadow grew, however, whenever

76

he was caught up in a situation where his modified Colt was drawn from its holster.

Clint also wanted to keep his name under his hat because it never failed to draw attention of the worst kind. As long as he answered to the name of Clint Adams, he would be known as The Gunsmith. And as long as there was a Gunsmith, there would be men out to gun him down just for the bragging rights.

With his name flowing through the ranch like the cold winter's breeze, all of Clint's fears in this regard were proven to be well founded. The shadow of The Gunsmith was bigger than ever and it was following him around morning, noon and night.

So far, the folks around the Double Briar didn't seem to be afraid of Clint. Although they were a little nervous, they were more grateful to have him around than anything else. That might change once the ambushes and shooting stopped, but for the moment Clint's shadow was doing some good.

The ranch now had the feel of a fort. There were armed men walking the perimeter, and patrols riding in and out through the front gates. Hank Ossutt was laid up in his house, nursing the leg and ankle that had been twisted on his last outing.

Mace was in that house as well, grumbling and snarling like a dog that wanted to get outside and stretch his legs. With those being the only injuries that they knew about, Clint figured the rancher and his workers were pretty damn lucky.

But there was still one injury that nobody knew for sure about.

Andy's body had yet to be found. By this point, after all that had already happened, a body was all anyone expected to find. That much wasn't said directly, but it was like another shadow looming over the entire ranch.

Folks only talked about Andy as if he'd been gone for a while and wasn't expected back. There was some hope in their words, but that's all it was: words. None of that hope showed through in anyone's eyes. By now, even Clint was well prepared to hear the worst about that missing man.

It was getting close to noon and Clint was leaning against the smokehouse where the prisoner was being held. He could hear the gunman rattling around in there, as well as a few pained grunts and groans. Every so often, the man would smack his fist against the wall, but he knew better than to try and step outside.

At least, for the moment.

The sound of light footsteps reached Clint's ears. With his senses still sharpened by the cold, he could also hear enough material rustling to figure that it was a woman who was approaching him from behind. The scent of rosewater proved him right, but when he turned around Clint was surprised by who he found.

"Lynne? What are you doing out here?"

Ossutt's daughter was dressed in a dark purple skirt that flowed out from the bottom of the coat that was tightly wrapped around her. From what could be seen beneath the collar of her coat, she was wearing several more layers which matched the color of her skirt. Her black hair flowed around her face, strands of it swirling in the breeze.

"Is he in there?" she asked, ignoring Clint's original question.

Clint looked back at the smokehouse and then to the young woman's face. Judging by the eagerness in her eyes, it was hard to tell whether she was there to see the man outside the smokehouse or the one trapped inside of it.

"He's still in there," Clint said. "At least, until they get finished over there." When he said that, Clint pointed over toward a storage shack less than twenty paces away. Several ranch hands worked inside the small shack, building it into a more suitable jail.

She glanced over to the workers, but didn't seem too interested in watching them fortify walls or put nails through lumber. Instead, she turned her attention back to Clint and said, "I've heard that you're something of a known man."

"Some might say that."

"Everybody's saying it. If half the things I've heard are true, it's lucky that you're here right about now."

"I'll do my best, but the men around here are doing a fine job on their own accord. I'm just lending a hand."

Hearing that, Lynne took her hands out of her pockets and reached out to Clint. She took hold of his right hand and rubbed it between her own. When she looked up at him, there was a spark in her eyes which sent a heat wave through both of them.

"Some hands are more capable than others," she said. "I wish I could have seen you take on those killers. I bet it was quite a sight."

Slowly, Clint eased his hand out of Lynne's grasp. "Your father was there," he said in a way to subtly test her.

Apparently, that was a test that Lynne was more than accustomed to. She smirked and pushed a few strands of hair from her face. "He's a brave man, but I've seen him stand his ground. I'm talking about seeing a man like you handle a gun. Even I've heard of The Gunsmith."

"You shouldn't believe everything you hear."

"I know. That's why I like to see things for myself. What's the matter, Clint?" she asked, stepping in a little closer. "Don't you like me?"

"Sure I do. It's just that this is the first time you've said more than three words to me since I've been here."

"I try to stay away from the men who pass through. It's safer that way. You've been around for a bit now, but you seem to be more interested in Percy."

It always took a moment for Clint to realize that Percy was Phoebe's name around the ranch. Some folks called her that because Percy was the only name of hers they

knew. Others did it out of habit. A few even did it because
they thought it got under Phoebe's skin.

This time, it seemed to be the latter.

"You think I've got my eyes on Percy?" Clint asked.

"Come on, Clint. It may be a big house, but I do live
there. I know you go in and out of her room at all hours.
That doesn't bother me. Maybe she's not the only one who
wants to spend some time with you."

"Is that why you came here?"

Smirking like a cat who'd just gotten a mouse under its
paw, Lynne shifted her eyes back to the smokehouse. "That
and to get a look at this one. I'd like to see just who's been
trying to run my family off this land."

"Hey, Clint," shouted one of the men working at the
nearby shack. "You can bring him on over whenever you're
ready."

Clint looked down into the brunette's eager eyes.
"Seems like your timing is impeccable."

TWENTY-ONE

Before Clint allowed the prisoner to step foot out of where he was being held, he wanted to inspect the new accommodations for himself. After posting one of the other men as a guard, he walked over to take a look at the renovated shack.

The small building had been used for storage, so it was already sturdy enough to withstand the elements. The ranch hands had nailed some hardier timber in place and sealed off the windows, which made the shack something close to a solid block of wood. There was even a post that had been sunk into the ground right in the middle of the room.

Satisfied by what he'd seen, Clint stepped out of the shack and nodded to the waiting workers. "Looks great. Can one of you scrounge up a cot and some more rope?"

"Sure thing, Mr. Adams," one of the men replied.

"All right, then. I'll bring our guest right over."

Hearing that was enough to bristle the hairs on the other men's necks. Clint had tried to keep them away from the prisoner more for the prisoner's sake. After everything that had happened, the ranch hands were plenty eager to sink their teeth into any one of the perpetrators.

That was how lynch mobs were born, and Clint wanted to stay out of that territory for as long as possible.

"Can I stay and watch?" Lynne asked.

Knowing that he probably wouldn't be able to deter her anyhow, Clint replied, "Only if you keep back a ways."

"I will. I promise."

"Then you'd best get moving."

Lynne moved away from the shack and stopped under a tall tree somewhere between both the shack and the smokehouse. The tree's bare branches hung low and swayed in the wind like skeletal fingers reaching down to protect her.

Signaling for two of the ranch hands to follow him, Clint walked toward the smokehouse's front door.

One of the men who went with Clint was a young kid with a mop of unruly red hair setting like a nest on top of his head. The boy's hair was so thick that it did better than a hat in keeping him warm. The second man was a lean figure with dark skin. His skin seemed even darker against the light gray of the sky behind him.

The black man was eager to work and had become one of the faces most familiar to Clint throughout his stay at the Double Briar. His name was Camden Ezerekiah, which was such a mouthful that everyone had taken to calling him Zeke.

Zeke was actually the first man Clint had wanted with him simply because he didn't seem overly eager to draw the gun at his side. When he stepped up beside Clint, Zeke was a strong presence who didn't need to say a word for Clint to trust him.

"Nobody makes a move unless I make it first," Clint said in a hushed tone. "You two understand me?"

Both men nodded.

"Get your guns out, but don't fire a shot unless I fire first."

"What if he gets the drop on you?" the redhead asked.

"Not even then," Clint said sternly enough to get another round of more serious nods in response.

Figuring that the other men were under control, Clint reached out and started unlocking the newly fortified smokehouse door. By the time the door was swinging open, there wasn't a sound coming from inside the place.

Clint knew damn well not to take any comfort from that.

"Come on out of there," Clint said into the smokehouse. When he didn't get a reply, he added, "If I have to come in there, I'm adding another bump to that head of yours."

That was all that needed to be said to get the prisoner to lurch forward into the light. "You're a real asshole, you know that?" the man grumbled.

"So I've been told," Clint said wryly. "Get moving."

"Where to now? You gonna toss me into a root cellar?"

"Actually, you've got your own little place to stay right over there."

When the prisoner saw where Clint was headed, he rolled his eyes and let out an exaggerated groan. "Jesus, you folks are a sorry bunch. I've been in real jails and you think this can hold me for long?"

"That's not very nice considering all the trouble we've gone to." Clint reached out and took hold of the rope binding the prisoner's hands together. He pulled the other man along with him as he started walking toward the shack. "And I'd watch what you say about these men. This sorry bunch dragged your ass into a smokehouse. What does that say about you?"

The prisoner decided not to respond to that. He also went along without much struggle, which was Clint's only real intention. As far as prisoner transfers were concerned, it wasn't any big deal. In Clint's mind, that was plenty good enough.

Once he'd taken a step into the shack, Clint pulled the

prisoner in as well and then pushed him toward the middle of the room. The other man wheeled around and almost fell over when his legs tested the limit of the rope that lashed them together. There wasn't much slack, but enough to allow the prisoner to keep his balance.

"Hold your hands down by that post," Clint ordered.

Despite the defiance in the prisoner's eyes, he did what he was told.

"Don't skimp on the knots, Red," Clint said to the redhead behind him. "Zeke, make sure our friend here doesn't get any big ideas."

As Clint and Zeke leveled their guns at the prisoner, the redhead knelt down and fastened the rope tied to the post around the rope between the prisoner's hands. The younger man's fingers worked so quickly that they were hard to follow without getting dizzy. In just over a minute, there were so many tight knots connecting the prisoner to the post that the rope looked more like a thick chain.

The redhead stood up and took hold of the knotted rope. He pulled up on it several times and didn't so much as loosen one of them. "It's solid," he said to the other two armed men. "As solid as I can make it."

"That's fine," Clint said. "Why don't you head back and see what Mr. Ossutt wants you to do next?"

By the look on his face, the redhead clearly wanted to stay where he was. But it was that same look, combined with the fire in his eyes, that made Clint want him to leave. Reluctantly, the redhead nodded and walked out of the shack.

The prisoner's eyes had followed the redhead and now stayed fixed on the shack's single doorway. Clint followed the man's gaze and found Lynne standing just outside and peeking in curiously. Her black hair formed something of a curtain around that side of the door and her brown eyes grew wider once she saw that she'd been spotted.

"If I say the right thing, do I get to climb on top of that

one?" the prisoner asked. When Lynne's gaze fell upon him, he winked and licked his lips.

"Zeke, how about you show her out of here?" Clint requested.

The black man nodded. "More than happy to."

Once Zeke and Lynne had gone, Clint and the prisoner were the only ones who remained. Clint leaned against a wall with his Colt holstered at his side. He fixed an intense stare onto the other man and showed him the smile of a hungry wolf.

"You ready to answer some questions?" Clint asked. "Or do you want to make this the longest day of your life?"

TWENTY-TWO

"I don't know if I like this," Hank muttered as he hobbled back and forth in front of a large picture window. "Not one bit."

The rancher had his leg in a splint and was using an old battered cane to move around on his own two feet. Although his leg hadn't been broken, it had gotten close enough to send a stabbing pain through his lower body every time he made a move.

His wife and one of the other women who worked there had done a fine job of patching him up. In fact, they'd gone a little overboard, knowing that it was only a matter of time before Hank refused to sit still for any more treatments.

Hank's wife was in her late forties and had long, chestnut hair she tied back with a plain ribbon. Her skirts were covered by a thick apron, and she draped a series of shawls over her shoulders to protect herself against the cold that seeped in beneath the doors. She now sat in one corner of the front parlor. Her self-appointed duty was to keep an eye on Hank without making that fact too obvious.

"You don't like what, Hank?" she asked. "The cane? You'll only need to use it for a little while."

"No," Hank grumbled. "Not the cane. All of it. All of what's happening."

"I don't think anyone likes it, but we're all dealing with it. You're not on your own, you know. Not by a long shot."

Opening his mouth to speak, Hank stopped short when he saw the continuous flow of people walking back and forth inside the house. He moved closer to his wife and then decided to sit down in the chair beside her. He dropped down with a grateful, albeit haggard, sigh.

"It's Adams," Hank said so only his wife could hear.

She stopped what she was doing and looked over to him. "What about him? I thought he was helping us."

"He is, Peg, he is. It's just that I don't want things to get worse because I've got . . . well . . . a man like him working for me."

"You mean a gunfighter?"

Hank twitched and reached out as if he was going to clap his hand over his wife's mouth. He made it about halfway before pulling his hand back and doing his best to look casual.

All the while, Peg looked at her husband with confusion on her face. "What's the matter? He is a gunfighter, isn't he?"

"Yes, but that's no reason to provoke him."

She held his gaze for a second, but was unable to hold back her smile for much longer than that. Once she allowed the smile onto her face, it was only a few short steps before she was actually laughing at her husband.

"I'm sorry," she said in response to Hank's shocked expression. "But you should hear yourself. You sound like a nervous old—" She stopped herself before going too far, straightened up and cleared her throat. "You sound nervous. Maybe you should have a sip of whiskey."

"I don't think that'd help, but you're right. I'm nervous as hell about all this. It's my fault that any of this happened."

"That's ridiculous. Why would it be your fault?"

"Because this is my land and those are my men. They're in danger because they're here, working for me."

Peg shook her head and got back to the sweater she was knitting. "This place might feel like a barracks right about now, but that doesn't mean you're a general. These men can leave whenever they want. Plenty of them have, you know."

Hank did know and, surprisingly enough, he didn't feel too bad about it. Peg always did know how to comfort him.

"Besides," she went on to say, "this won't last too much longer. Once the law gets here to take things over, it'll be out of your hands and we can get back to normal. We've dealt with rustlers before and they always get scared off once they see that we're not backing down."

Hank was quiet as he stared through the window at all the activity going on outside.

"You've always done everything you could to keep this ranch going and to protect everyone who counts on you," Peg went on to say. "As long as you keep doing that, everything will work out just fine."

Even though his wife seemed comforted by the truth in what she'd said, that peace didn't quite make it onto Hank's face. Instead, he still stared out the window.

His brow furrowed and he pulled in a weary breath.

When he let that breath out, his eyes looked haunted and his heart sank a little deeper in his chest.

TWENTY-THREE

Clint stepped out of the makeshift jail around twenty minutes after he'd first gone in. The redhead and Zeke were waiting in the spots where they should have been, and Lynne was standing among them as well. As soon as Clint stepped through the door, all three of the others snapped their eyes toward him.

"What happened in there?" Zeke asked. "Did you get him to say anything?"

Clint closed the door and was extra careful to make sure every latch was in place and every lock was closed tightly. It was a patchwork job, but more than sturdy enough to keep one man inside.

"Did you make him talk?" the redhead asked, unable to hide the hopeful tone in his voice. "Should I get some bandages?"

Although she'd started off just as intent as the others, Lynne's face dropped a bit the longer she watched Clint go about the task of closing and locking the door. When he turned around again, she stepped forward so she could look straight into his eyes.

"Clint?" she asked. "What's the matter?"

Some of the color had drained from Clint's face. He

didn't look frightened, so much as he looked rattled. Even though they'd only known him for a short while, all three knew that Clint Adams wasn't the type to get rattled by much of anything.

Glancing quickly at the falling expressions on the faces around him, Clint quickly walked away from the door and made sure the others followed. Looking over to the red-head, Clint said, "You stay put and make sure he doesn't so much as raise his voice too loud. You understand me?"

The redhead nodded quickly.

"He makes any trouble, you take care of it," Clint said for emphasis. "He gets too far out of line, knock him in the head again. You shouldn't have to hit him too hard to put him down for a while."

The redhead nodded again. After seeing the intensity in Clint's eyes and hearing the firmness in his tone, he took the orders as if they'd been handed down by The Almighty himself.

Clint saw that some of the eagerness had gone out of the redhead's face as well. At this point, however, that was the least of his concerns.

"Zeke," Clint said once he and the other two put some distance between themselves and the shack, "come with me. Lynne, you shouldn't be staying around here. There's plenty that could go wrong."

"But I can help," she said defiantly. "I can—"

"You can be a big help, but when you're right here at this moment, you're just hoping to get a look at something exciting or catch sight of a fight. You have no idea how stupid that is right now."

Lynne's face hardened instantly. "Stupid? Nobody talks to me like that."

"Do you realize that men have been shot for being in the wrong place at the wrong time?" Clint asked. "Men have died who know their way around a fight a hell of a lot bet-ter than you do. If you want to split hairs about the tone in my voice, that's up to you. Or you can trust me when I say that you need to get out of the open and help out where you can really do some good."

Although her temper had flared a few moments ago, Lynne now realized that she was more angry with how he'd said them than the words themselves. His tone had softened a bit, which gave her a moment to realize that he wasn't exactly speaking out of turn.

"All right," she said with a nod. "I'll go. But I'll be coming back out to check on everyone. It's part of my job here."

Clint walked with her for a few steps and reached out to take hold of her elbow. The brunette made a show of trying to get away from him, but allowed herself to be pulled back until she was practically pressed against Clint's chest.

"You're a strong woman," Clint said to her. "Don't let that keep you from seeing when it's best to lay low and let others step in on your behalf." Focusing on her eyes even more, he added, "Folks around here can benefit from that strength. Put it to good use."

The defiance on Lynne's face melted away until it was nothing more than a shell. That shell cracked for good once she lowered her head and nodded. "You're right. But come back to let me know what's going on. If not right now, promise you'll tell me soon."

"I will."

"Promise me, Clint."

"I promise."

Lynne started to move away from him. Before she took a full step back, she leaned in and planted a quick kiss on his lips. The kiss was as warm as it was fast and left Clint with a definite, unspoken promise that there was plenty more where that had come from.

"That's just to make sure you come back to see me," she whispered.

With that, Lynne turned and walked toward the main

house. There was a confidence in her stride that showed through in every step. She didn't even have to look over her shoulder to know Clint was watching her. There simply wasn't an alternative.

Once he was able to take his eyes away from Lynne's slender figure, Clint shook his head and made his way back to where Zeke was waiting. When he saw the smirk on Zeke's face, Clint knew that the other man had a real good idea of what was happening in regards to the rancher's daughter.

"Is she always like that?" Clint asked.

"Nah. Most the times, she's worse."

Certain that he and the other man were out of anyone else's earshot, Clint asked, "How long have you worked here, Zeke?"

The black man thought for a moment before replying, "About six or seven months."

"Was that enough time to get a good feel for some of the men you work with?"

"Sure. It doesn't take long for that."

"You think you can pull together a few who you trust with your life?"

After a brief pause, Zeke nodded. "I can think of one or two I can trust."

"Good. We're going to need as many as we can get."

TWENTY-FOUR

"I've been real patient since you got finished talking to that man in there," Zeke said to Clint. "I was even patient when I was helping to build a jail in the middle of this here ranch. But I'll tell you something, Mr. Adams. My patience is starting to wear mighty thin."

Clint had been leading Zeke across the ranch without saying much of anything. He'd asked Zeke to help him walk the perimeter to make sure everything was safe, which was exactly what Zeke had done without squawking once.

Now, with their path about to bring them full circle, Zeke planted his feet and refused to take another step. "You've asked me a whole lot of things and I've done my best to answer. It's about time I get some answers for myself."

"You're right," Clint said as he came to a stop.

Clint's quick and decisive answer seemed to have caught Zeke a little off-guard. He quickly nodded and placed his hands on his hips. "Yeah, I'm right."

"What do you want to know?"

"First off, I'd like to know the answer to the question I asked a while back. Just what the hell happened between you and that prisoner?"

93

Clint and Zeke were at the fence that surrounded the main cluster of buildings at the center of Ossutt's land. The house, as well as all the other major structures, were easy enough to see. Although there were men walking about and riding out to the farther acres of land, all of them were too busy to take much notice of two figures having a talk.

This was exactly as Clint had planned it, despite the fact that he'd seemed to just come to a stop and settle in where he and Zeke had landed.

"That prisoner and I had a chat," Clint explained. "It took a little convincing, but he eventually decided to stop acting tough and start doing what I asked."

"How much . . . convincing did it take?"

Clint shook his head, comforted by the other man's discomfort with the thought of getting too rough with the captured gunman. There seemed to be way too many like the redhead who were all too eager to draw blood. "I didn't need to do anything like that," Clint said. "I already felt bad enough about cracking him over the head."

Zeke was relieved to hear that, but still a little confused. "How'd you get him to talk?"

"The same way I'd get a man to fold a pair of aces when all I've got is a busted straight."

"You bluffed him?"

"That's right."

Zeke nodded. "I like your style, Mr. Adams."

"Please, call me Clint. That's what you called me when I was working here before."

"That was before anyone knew who you truly was."

"I'm still the same man. Only now, folks know my last name. Anyway, once our guest got rolling, he had plenty to say . . ."

The air inside the makeshift jail still smelled like a mixture of the items that had been stored there. It wasn't anything that could be nailed down in particular, but more of a general musty flavor that could be found in any attic or closet. Some of those things were still littered about, but none of them were within reach of the man tied to the middle of the floor.

The prisoner had already tugged a few times on the rope holding him to the post, but those knots were like clamps and weren't about to budge anytime soon. Clint and the prisoner had already exchanged some unpleasant words, which had resulted in a kind of stalemate.

Clint's last words had definitely left the prisoner rattled.

"You ready to answer some questions?" Clint had asked. "Or do you want to make this the longest day of your life?"

"What questions?" the prisoner asked, doing a bad job at keeping up his gruff show.

"Let's start with who you are."

"The name's Nick. That's all you need to know."

"At least I've got something to call you. Now tell me, Nick. Why were you ambushing a bunch of ranchers when you could probably have just as easily snuck by them?"

"You're no rancher, Adams. I've heard enough to know that."

"But you didn't know that at the time, did you?" Clint paused for a moment to study the other man's face. "No. My guess is you didn't, so that brings us right back to where we started."

"You want to know who we are? You'd best ask the owner of this here ranch."

"You mean Hank Ossutt?"

"That's the one."

"What does he know about any of this?"

Nick gave the post in the ground one last kick before dropping down and sitting next to it. "Will came by to have a word with him before any of this happened."

"Will who?"

Wincing as if he'd been unpleasantly surprised to hear

himself mention that name, Nick looked down at the ground and grumbled, "Will Dreyer. He's the one who came by here."

That name struck Clint like a fist in the jaw. The last time he'd heard it had been in Omaha before he'd set out west. At the time, the name hadn't been familiar. His name had only been mentioned once or twice in connection to the gang of killers that was supposedly wreaking havoc across two states. When Clint had moved on, he figured he'd keep the name in the back of his mind in case he happened to come across it again.

It seemed that that time had come.

"How long ago did Will Dreyer come here?" Clint asked.

"More'n a month. I'm not sure, exactly."

"Go on," Clint ordered as he watched the other man with sharp, focused eyes.

"He came by to offer Hank a deal. It wasn't even a bad deal compared to some of the others he'd offered to folks before. All Will wanted was to cross through this here property without having to answer to anyone."

"And without anyone telling the law where he was going?"

Nick shrugged and nodded.

"What else?"

"Some traveling money. A few head of cows. It was a tax for Will and the rest of us to leave everything else alone. Hell, it was a better deal than the others got."

"And what if he refused?"

"Oh, he refused all right," Nick said without hesitation. "That's why we came back." Despite being bloodied and tied to a post in a jail built especially for him, the prisoner was getting bolder with every word that came out of his mouth. "And that's why they'll keep coming back so they can free me, kill all of you, take all that old man has and burn this ranch to the ground."

Clint could tell he was losing his leverage with the prisoner, so he decided to make one last play before the man called his bluff. Reaching down to grab hold of Nick by the lapels of his jacket, Clint lifted the other man partly off the ground.

"You said you offered this deal to others," Clint snarled. "What others?"

Nick grinned like a devil in Clint's face. "You ever hear of a place called Ambling Creek?"

TWENTY-FIVE

Zeke blinked as Clint mentioned that last name. "Ambling Creek?"

"Right," Clint said. "Ever hear of it?"

"Sure. It's not much of a town, but it's not bad. I stayed at a hotel there when I was on my way here from Omaha. There's a mighty nice cathouse right next to the saloon."

"Well, there's not much of anything there anymore."

"What?"

Clint nodded. "I passed through there on my way here also. There wasn't much of anything left but empty buildings and deserted streets."

After a moment, Zeke shook his head. "That can't be right. You must've gone to the wrong place."

"No. I was at the right place. The only problem is that the place wasn't there anymore. According to Nick, Ambling Creek was gutted and burned to the ground by this fellow Will Dreyer and his bunch."

"How could that happen?" Zeke asked in disbelief. "Why would someone do that?"

"I'd heard about a group of killers cutting back and forth across the state line back when I was in Omaha. There were plenty of stories going around about them, but nothing more than that as far as I could tell. I thought it was just another bunch of rumors surrounding some group of kids with more guns than brains.

"A lawman out that way mentioned the name Will Dreyer, but I had never heard of it before. Since there wasn't much of anything going on that I could see, I tucked the name in the back of my head and moved on."

"And this Dreyer fellow is the one who's been leading these ambushes on the Double Briar?" Zeke asked.

Clint nodded, craning his neck to watch everything that was going on around him. Although his eyes and ears were constantly searching for anything out of the ordinary, the rest of him was taking a moment to relax. It was the longest rest he'd had since he'd opened his eyes that morning.

After glancing nervously toward the renovated shack and back again, Zeke said, "I thought you tracked down killers like these. Some folks say you're a gunslinger, but I've heard different. I've heard that you sign on with lawmen or even regular folks who need help."

"I lend a hand where I can."

"Then why didn't you back in Omaha?"

Clint shifted his eyes so they could stare directly into Zeke's. "Because nobody asked me, that's why. I didn't see anyone get hurt, and as far as I knew, there wasn't even much of anything to this gang than some rumors that they probably started on their own."

For a moment, Zeke still seemed to be worked up. He then let the breath out that he'd been holding and nodded. "You're right. Sorry about that."

Then Clint spotted something else in the other man's eyes. "Did you know someone in Ambling Creek?"

Slowly, Zeke nodded again. It was a sad, solemn nod. "Yeah. My uncle and his family lived there. They lived there all their lives. Did that bastard in there tell you what they did to the folks in Ambling Creek?"

"No," Clint replied. "Just that they ran them off and

rode through town like wild bulls taking as much as they could carry. That's most of what this whole gang does. They call themselves the Reapers."

"Why did they pick Ambling Creek?" Zeke muttered to himself. "Why a little place like that? They didn't even have much of anything to steal."

"They didn't pick Ambling Creek," Clint said. "It was just on their way. It was hardly the only town to get hit like that. I rode through at least three others before I got here, myself."

"Three others?"

Clint nodded. "Towns dry up and blow away quick enough on their own sometimes, especially nowadays. I thought it was strange to hit four in a row, but just figured it was a run of bad luck. Turns out that I was hardly the one to get the bad luck."

Zeke was still shaking his head in disbelief. "You mean to tell me this gang rides through and wipes out whole towns?"

"I didn't get too close a look at all the ones I found," Clint replied. "But I doubt I can believe everything that comes out of our guest's mouth. More than likely, it's a combination of the gang wreaking havoc and folks just pulling up stakes and leaving because of it. With towns that size, it's easier to move along than deal with a bunch of rowdy gunmen."

"Especially when you're just a family of honest folks who only want to make a quiet living." Zeke seemed to be talking to himself again, but he quickly focused in on Clint. "I need to get to Ambling Creek. No matter what's left, I need to get there and see it for myself."

Zeke was building up steam with each passing second. "My uncle could still be there. Maybe some others are, too. And if they're not . . ." He paused and took a breath as his face darkened considerably. "I still need to go there, so don't try and stop me."

"I wouldn't dream of stopping you," Clint said. "In fact, I was going to ask if you could come with me when I rode back there to get another look for myself. Now that I know what I'm looking for, I might be able to get a better grip on what we're up against."

At first, Zeke looked a bit surprised. Then he smiled and nodded. "I'd be honored to ride with you, Mr. Adams. I mean, Clint. But what about Mr. Ossutt? He needs all the help he can get right here."

"And there's plenty of people to help him right here. If we can figure out what kind of threat we're taking on, we'll help him more than we could here. Besides, it would be good to know if these Reapers are more bark than bite."

"Sounds like they might be."

"Then we need to know that. Every little bit of knowledge we can get will help."

"I agree. When do we ride?"

"As soon as we get some supplies together and saddle up. But first, I need to have a word with Hank about his missing man."

"Andy?" Zeke asked as his face brightened. "You know where he is? Is he all right?"

"He's alive, but according to what I was told, he's anything but all right."

TWENTY-SIX

Hank was on his feet and hobbling toward the door before Clint had a chance to step all the way through it. The ranch had settled down a bit in the late afternoon, but the house itself was still buzzing with activity. Most of that was due to the ranch's owner, who shouted orders and spoke personally with every hand who came in from patrol.

"Adams!" Hank bellowed. "I saw your horse being saddled up and brought out from the stables. You heading out on your patrol early?"

"Not quite. I'm heading out to do some scouting, and Zeke's coming with me."

"Scouting? Zeke's going with you? What the hell is this? I didn't order any of that!"

"Well, it's necessary and if you have a seat and listen to me, I'll tell you why."

Despite the sweat on his brow and wince on his face, Hank said, "I think I'll stand, thank you very much."

"Suit yourself."

Clint stayed on his feet as well, as he told the rancher everything that had been told to him by the man being held prisoner in the Double Briar's new jail. Hank listened to the whole account without interrupting once. Every so often, he looked like he was about to explode into some kind of outburst, but managed to hold his temper.

And while he spoke to the rancher, Clint was busy keeping a close eye on every one of Hank's reactions. Earlier, Clint had mentioned to Zeke that important conversations were like playing a game of poker. This one was no different and Clint was still looking for the tells on Hank's face that would let him know what cards the rancher might be holding.

When he mentioned the Reapers, Clint noticed that Hank seemed surprised and outraged. Perhaps he was a little too surprised and outraged. All in all, the rancher struck Clint as a mediocre actor doing his best to stay in character.

When he mentioned Andy's name, however, Clint knew that Hank's surprise was genuine.

"You heard something about Andy?" Hank asked, stepping forward so quickly that a stab of pain from his twisted knee almost took him down. He sucked in a breath and tried to ignore his stumble. "What happened to Andy? Where is he?"

"I don't know exactly where he is," Clint replied. "I do know that he's probably alive."

"That's great news."

"Just wait until you hear the rest of it."

Hank's expression froze upon his face, but he was obviously eager to hear what Clint had to say.

Clint focused on the rancher's face even harder, watching for what could be the biggest tell of all. "Andy's a traitor."

After a moment of stunned silence, Hank asked, "What was that?"

"He works for Will Dreyer and his Reapers."

"That prisoner must've been lying to save his own skin. Or maybe he was just making that up to throw you off the track."

"I don't think he was," Clint said. "Just like I don't think the Reapers being here is much of a surprise to you."

Hank's eyes snapped back onto Clint, displaying an angry spark. He held the fire in his gaze for a solid couple of seconds, but when he saw that Clint wasn't budging, Hank averted his eyes. "Maybe I will sit down," he said while letting out a tired breath.

Peg stepped into the room when she saw her husband lower himself carefully onto a chair. "Are you all right, Hank?" she asked.

"I'm fine," the rancher said quickly. "Let me and Clint talk in peace."

She didn't seem to take offense at the biting way Hank spoke. Instead, she looked to Clint in a way that silently asked him to keep an eye on her husband. Only after Clint nodded back to her did she leave them in the room by themselves.

"It's been eating me up inside," Hank grumbled.

Clint stepped up beside the rancher and took the seat next to him. "How long have you known about the Reapers?"

"A few months," Hank replied with a shake of his head. It seemed as though the man had aged another ten years in the time it took for him to lower himself down onto his padded seat. "Will Dreyer and a few of his boys showed up on my land asking for some water. It was during a hot spell and I obliged without thinking too much of it.

"They didn't even stay the night and didn't ask for any work, so I figured they'd be moving on. Then Will comes right up to me like he was cock of the walk and says I need to pay him five thousand dollars or he'd see to it that I was sorry."

"Do you have that kind of money around here?"

Hank shook his head. "And I told him that much. He said I could hand over whatever I had and pay the rest off in pieces."

Nodding, Clint added, "With interest, I'm sure."

"You could say that. I was to let him know when cattle buyers were stopping by, where I was meeting them, or when any other business associates were due to pay me a visit."

"Anyone with money."

"That's right."

"What did you tell him?"

"I told him to go to hell," Hank snarled. "And that's when he told me that I was making a big mistake and I'd pay for it." Hank gritted his teeth and clenched his hand into a tight fist. "Andy came to work for me a few weeks later. Was he sent by Will Dreyer?"

Clint nodded. "That's what the prisoner said and I tend to believe him. It seems to fit."

"It makes sense that they'd send someone to get familiar with this place and the men here. Dammit, I was stupid in taking him in like that."

"How were you supposed to know?"

"I don't know, but I should've known anyway. Maybe we wouldn't be in such a predicament right now."

Standing up, Clint replaced his hat on his head. "All that's left now is for us to make the best of what we've got, and that's exactly what I intend on doing."

"I wish to hell I could get my hands on Andy just one more time."

"You'll probably get your chance before too long. But don't stop sending out those men to look for him."

"Why? I could use all the men I've got close to my family. What if those Reapers come through here and all my men are spread out from here to Texas?"

"If that happens, it's probably best that your men are spread out a bit. They mean well, but they're not experienced gunhands. Well, not all of them anyway. Covering a wider area will allow you to see anyone else coming much sooner. Besides, bringing them in will probably only tip off Dreyer that his mole has been dug up."

"You think he knows what's going on in here?" Hank asked. "Even though Andy's gone?"

"Just because you can't see him doesn't mean he's gone. Besides, there might be another man already taking his place. Either way, it's safer to assume Dreyer knows something about what's going on here."

"Jesus. What the hell am I gonna do?"

"You're going to be thankful that we're one step ahead of the game," Clint replied sternly. "And you're going to make sure that prisoner stays under lock and key and doesn't get a chance to talk to anyone. At least he's one loose end that we can keep our eyes on. Other than that, make sure your men are looking for Dreyer and any of his men while they're out on patrol. That's still going to be a big help."

"What about you?"

"I won't be gone long. In the meantime, send someone out to get help from the law or anywhere else. We're going to need it."

TWENTY-SEVEN

Clint strode out of the house and headed straight to his Darley Arabian stallion, which was ready and waiting for him. Both the horse and the rider seemed anxious to get moving and were already doing so before both of Clint's feet were firmly in the stirrups. Zeke and his horse had been waiting outside and were just as eager to go.

Once both men started riding away from the house, they picked up some speed. Once they got clear of the gate opening onto the rest of Ossutt's land, they took off like they were in a race.

Watching them ride off, Lynne Ossutt held her arms crossed over the front of her body. She stood in the front room of the house, which happened to be the hub of activity for most of the ranch. Armed men were coming and going, workers were bustling here and there, even Lynne's mother was rushing about like her skirt was on fire.

Although they saw she was standing there, most people walked past her without much thought. Under normal circumstances, being all but ignored like that might have annoyed her. But these weren't normal circumstances. In fact, Lynne was more than happy to go unnoticed.

She felt another blast of cold tear through her as another

man pushed by and stepped outside. Stepping to one side, she pulled back the curtains covering one of the front windows so she could get a better look out.

Clint and Zeke were practically specks on the horizon, and growing smaller by the second. Considering what she'd overheard in her father's study not too long ago, she didn't think either of those other two men would be turning back anytime soon.

"Lynne, honey, I need you to fetch some water for me," said her mother from the dining room, which had practically been changed into a saloon to serve hot drinks to all the ranch hands.

The young woman was well practiced in the art of ignoring her parents, and even more skilled at moving about the house without drawing too much attention. Keeping her head down, she wove between the men standing around, until she got to a narrow staircase that led to the second floor.

Lynne was careful to avoid the squeaky boards as she dashed up the stairs, even though that much precaution probably wasn't necessary. Once she made it off the first floor, she was in the clear. Only a few others moved around up there and they were either family or those who normally worked closest to the Ossutts.

"Watch where you're going," came a smooth, yet firm voice in the hall.

Lynne's eyes snapped up from where they'd been focused to find a familiar face looking at her from one of the open doorways. While Lynne might have been good at sneaking around her own home, Phoebe was even better. In fact, the maid could go unnoticed much more often than the owner of the Double Briar.

"Percy," Lynne said in a snapping tone. "You startled me."

"Sorry about that. I was just gathering some linens and clothes to be cleaned. Not that I don't already have more than I can handle already."

"Right, well go on ahead, then." Saying that, Lynne stepped to one side so she could press her back against the wall. An exasperated expression hung on her face, as though the act of moving to let Phoebe pass was physically exhausting.

Shaking her head at the exaggerated eye rolling coming from Lynne, Phoebe walked past the young woman and headed toward the stairs. She knew better than to ask her for any help with the load of clothes and linens that spilled over both of her arms. The heaping pile was almost bigger than the woman carrying it, but Phoebe lugged it all with practiced ease.

"Is there anything else you want up here?" Lynne asked in an unapologetically snippy tone.

"No, I've got plenty to keep me busy."

"Good. I mean," Lynne paused and plastered a wide, unconvincing smile onto her face, "just let me know if you need any help."

"Sure," Phoebe said. After she'd turned and started walking down the stairs, she grumbled, "As if you'd actually lift anything besides that dress of yours."

Lynne didn't hear a word of that. She was already in her own room, closing the door and leaning back against it with a breathless sigh. "Finally, I made it out of all that noise. If I had to wait any longer before getting up here, I thought I was going to burst."

"Yeah," Andy said as he got up from where he'd been sitting and walked over to her. "I know just what you mean."

TWENTY-EIGHT

Andy looked like a far cry from the man who'd parted ways with Kyle and was never heard from again. By the looks of him, one might have thought that he'd been through more than a few battles of his own in the time that everyone else had been looking for him. His youthful face was dirty and covered in scruff and his clothes were a rumpled mess stretched across his back.

"Damn, girl, you're a sight for sore eyes," Andy said as he moved forward and swept Lynne up into his arms.

The young woman wrapped her arms around him as well, kicking both feet up behind her as Andy picked her up off the floor. She giggled breathlessly as she was twirled about before finally being set back down on her own two feet.

Her smile turned from happy to lustful in the blink of an eye. As soon as she felt Andy's hands slide around her waist, Lynne leaned her head back slightly and closed her eyes in expectation of Andy's kiss. She didn't have to wait long, as Andy leaned in to press his mouth against hers. His hands moved up and down along her back as both of their breathing started to pick up.

Andy took hold of her with both hands, feeling the

curve of her hips as well as the gentle slope of her back. From there, he eased his hands down to cup her tight, perfectly round little backside. Her buttocks filled his hands just right, and when he felt the soft curves, he let out a bit of a laugh himself.

"Lord, it's been too long," he said. "I've been dreaming about this for days!"

Lynne was savoring the strength of Andy's hands on her body as she started nibbling his ear. "Feels more like months," she whispered. "Years, maybe. Everyone's been looking for you, running around here like a bunch of fools."

Already pulling her skirt up so he could slip his hand between her legs, Andy grunted, "None of these assholes would know their ass from a hole in the ground."

"You've made fools of them all, baby," she groaned as Andy's fingers slipped over the soft silk of her panties. "Even Clint Adams, himself."

Andy's hand froze where it was. His breath caught in the back of his throat. "Clint Adams? What made you bring up that name?"

"Because he's here, baby. Everyone knows that."

"The hell they do," Andy snarled as he roughly pulled his hand out from beneath Lynne's dress. "I didn't know about it."

"You didn't?"

"How the hell would I know anything? I'm cooped up in here, hiding from that bitch maid, and before that I was holed up in the weeds like some goddamn prairie dog."

Lynne wasn't thrown off too much by the angry tone that had suddenly gotten into Andy's voice. Instead, her hands were moving twice as fast on him, as if to pick up the extra slack.

"Ooo, that sounds so terrible," she whispered while reaching down to unbuckle his belt. "Sleeping all alone in the cold." Her hands pulled his pants open and quickly slid right down inside the front of them. "Let me make you feel better."

The touch of Lynne's fingers against his bare flesh managed to calm Andy somewhat. There was still anger in his eyes, but it was holding up about as well as the flame on a candle inside a windy room. "It probably ain't even Adams. Not for real."

"It's him all right," she said while looking deeply into Andy's eyes. "I talked to him myself."

"Jesus Christ, this ain't good at all," Andy groaned as he started to pull away from Lynne.

But she wasn't about to let him go so easily. Rather than take her hands out of his pants, she pushed them further between his legs until she was able to cup his balls while wrapping the fingers of her other hand around the shaft of his penis. From there, she started stroking slowly while keeping her eyes locked on him the entire time.

"What about that?" she whispered. "Is that good?"

Moments ago, there had been an expression on Andy's face that was like a shadow creeping over him. Now that shadow was melting away and he was slowly letting out the breath that had caught in the back of his throat.

"Yeah," he sighed. "That's real good."

Lynne could feel him growing harder with every stroke. The feel of him stiffening in her hand made her own breathing speed up a bit. Soon, she was stepping closer to him, until she was able to press herself against him. As her hands worked below his waist, they now also brushed against her own body whenever she moved them along the tip of his cock.

"I've missed you," she purred. "It's been too long."

Andy knew that it hadn't been more than a week since the last time he'd been able to slip into Lynne's room. At least, he knew that on some level. At the moment, he was having trouble forming thoughts any more complex than where he was now and the shiver Lynne was sending through him.

"Way too long," Andy said. Once those two words left his mouth, he reached out and took hold of Lynne by the shoulders.

Although she jumped a bit at the sudden, rough way he grabbed her, the look on Lynne's face made it plain to see that she didn't mind it one bit. In fact, when Andy started tugging at her skirts and pulling them up around her waist, Lynne smiled and leaned her head back, savoring the moment.

Andy had plenty of troubles to think about and plenty of worries to occupy his mind. He'd even found something else that stuck like a burr under his saddle, but all of that was forgotten for now.

Right now, he had better things to do.

Lynne was more than enough to keep any man occupied.

TWENTY-NINE

Lynne's back hit her mattress with a solid thump. She let out a breath that was part grunt and part moan. Hearing the noise echo in the room made Andy perk up and look toward the door as though he expected it to be kicked in at any second. His attention was brought back to her, however, once his head was turned by one of Lynne's hands.

"Don't worry about any of them out there," Lynne gasped while wrapping her legs around him. "We could probably run a herd of buffalo through this room and nobody would notice."

That was more than enough to satisfy Andy's concern. Any others that he might have had disappeared like smoke once he got a look at the way Lynne was laying directly beneath him.

She'd tugged her shirt open and pulled open the corset underneath to reveal smooth, pale skin and small, perky breasts. Her pink nipples were the size of pennies and became rigid with one touch of her lover's hand. A shudder rippled through her when Andy started teasing the sensitive flesh with his fingers.

After allowing him to pleasure her like that for another few seconds, Lynne opened her eyes and took hold of

Andy by the front of his shirt. With strength that was surprising from someone of her size, she pulled Andy down and to one side until he flopped onto the bed beside her. Without taking her hands from him, she rolled on top with a satisfied grin.

"You know what I want," she said in an almost challenging voice.

Andy's eyes grew wide, but not as wide as his smile. "You ain't the only one who likes it, darlin'."

Pulling her skirt up and bunching it at her stomach, Lynne straddled Andy's chest and turned around so he could see her back. She then scooted toward Andy's face and spread her legs wider until she felt his mouth brushing against the inside of her thighs.

Lynne arched her back and let out a slow moan as Andy's mouth worked its way along the smooth flesh of her legs and to the even smoother skin between them. The moment she felt his tongue flick against her pussy, Lynne let out a little squeal.

Beneath her, Andy smirked and ran both hands up along the smooth, perfect curve of her buttocks. Lynne's backside fit perfectly in his grasp. It was small, yet perfectly round; something he'd always admired about her even before he'd gotten her into bed.

Lynne squirmed impatiently until she felt Andy pull her down lower so he could peel aside her panties. The damp material clung to her like a second skin. The effort of getting them off was more than worth it, however, once Andy was able to slip his tongue along the soft, moist lips of her vagina.

Lynne sat bolt upright. She wanted to cry out, but knew better than to push her luck since they were still inside her father's house. Also, her pleasure was so close to the surface that she couldn't have made a sound if she'd wanted to. Andy's tongue moved in practiced strokes.

It wasn't so much that he was a great lover, but he did

take direction fairly well. He kissed her the way she'd taught him, touched her the way she'd taught him and now licked her the way she'd taught him. For that, she figured he should be rewarded.

As Andy's head wriggled between her legs, Lynne reached down and pulled off his pants. His penis was rigid and felt like a stick of candy when she wrapped her lips around it. She bobbed her head up and down, feeling his body tense beneath her.

The moment that he felt her mouth wrap around his cock, Andy also felt his heart slam inside his chest. She worked her mouth over him so well that it damn near took his breath away. Her tongue swirled around the tip of his cock and she devoured every inch of him, as if she couldn't get enough.

Lynne could tell that Andy was getting close to climax, so she took her mouth away and slid her hand up and down along his column of flesh. That was enough to get his mind back on track, and soon Andy's tongue was again working its magic between her legs. She slowly moved her hips back and forth, leading him to the spots where she wanted him to go, as if he was an extension of her own hand.

As much as Andy wanted to be inside of her, he didn't dare stop what he was doing. Just when he thought he might take control, he felt her touch him in just the right spot or moan in just the right way, which was enough of an incentive for him to keep going. Besides, she tasted sweet against his lips and the thought of his rigid penis slipping into her pretty little mouth was practically enough to drive him out of his mind.

Leaning forward and stretching out with both arms, Lynne started crawling down Andy's body like a cat along a narrow branch. Her hands wrapped around his legs and slid down toward his ankles.

Although Andy missed the feel of her mouth and hand on him, the show he was getting went a long way in making up for it. Lynne's pert little backside twitched from side to side as her black hair spilled down her shoulders and back. When she stopped, she arched her sweet ass into the air and looked back at him over her shoulder, framing the wet lips between her legs perfectly.

Andy could feel his erection growing until it started to hurt. He grabbed hold of her ankles simply because that was the only part of her that he could easily reach. Before he could do anything else, he saw Lynne lift herself up slightly and lower herself down again.

With a few gentle shifts and a little more wriggling, Lynne fit Andy's cock into just the right spot. When she lowered herself down, she took him inside of her with a long, throaty moan. Lynne's eyes were closed and she tossed her hair back over one shoulder. Her hands gripped onto Andy's legs.

Although the weight of Lynne's body was enough to trap Andy where he was, there wasn't any reason for him to want to leave. He reached out and grabbed hold of the mattress, savoring the feel of her rocking back and forth on top of him.

Almost as good as that feeling was the view of her moving on top of him. She was beautiful from any angle, but from behind, she was a work of art. The curve of her spine was an easy line that traced down her back. Her shoulders undulated as she rode him and she shifted her weight so she could rub her clit against his solid penis.

Just above the slope of her buttocks, there were two little dimples that served to accentuate her already exquisite figure. And then Andy's eyes were drawn back to her backside, round and plump as ever.

Smiling contentedly, he laced his fingers behind his head, leaned back and enjoyed the ride. Even though she wasn't looking at him, Andy knew that Lynne was smiling, too. The sounds she made were enough to make that obvious.

And she definitely was smiling. Lynne's eyes were still shut, and every now and then she would twitch as a jolt of pleasure went through her body. Her firm little breasts wiggled back and forth as she sped up her pace. Her nipples became hard once again as she let her mind wander a ways from where she was.

While sliding up and down over her lover's cock, Lynne thought back to Clint Adams. He wouldn't need to be taught anything. She knew that just by looking at him. In fact, Lynne wagered that someone like Adams might even be able to teach her a thing or two.

As if proving her theory correct, Andy started to twitch and grunt beneath her. His orgasm was racing up onto him and, as usual, it was way ahead of Lynne's. He squirmed and started making his noises until his legs started twitching in Lynne's hands.

Ignoring him, she forced herself to think about what she would do to Clint Adams if it was him in her bed right now. She thought about what that stupid maid Percy had gotten that had put the smile on her face so many mornings.

She thought about that big gun at Clint's side and how many men had been cut down by it. She tried to imagine how many men had come after Adams and had only gotten a shallow grave for their troubles.

Men like Andy.

Lynne's hand had wandered down her stomach, tracing a familiar path that was usually only taken when she was alone. Her fingertips quickly found the spot above her clitoris and then slipped a bit further until she was pressing against that sensitive flesh.

Andy was starting to squirm even more, but it wasn't quite the same as when he'd been pumping up into her. Now he seemed to be trying to get her off of him.

But Lynne wasn't going to be moved. Not just yet.

Her finger was circling her clit and then finally rubbed back and forth against it as she thought even more about all the things that Clint Adams could do. Once she thought of him pressing that cold gun against her bare skin, she had to bite down on her lower lip to keep from screaming.

The orgasm was powerful. One of the biggest ones she'd had. It was an explosion compared to the little pops that Andy had given her.

"Jesus Christ," Andy wheezed. "You almost killed me, but it was damn good."

Lynne crawled off of him and slipped into her clothes. Her hand lingered between her legs, but she knew that Andy wouldn't notice. He was already asleep.

THIRTY

Clint hadn't exactly been meandering when he'd first passed through those empty towns and found his way to the Double Briar. At the time, he'd been taking the best route he could come up with and wasted as little time as possible. Even so, heading straight back to what was left of Ambling Creek, Clint felt that he must have been lost the first time around.

The ride back to that town seemed to take about half as long as before. Of course, he knew that difference was on account of two very important things. First of all, he was traveling in a straight line. Second, he had a guide with him who'd made that ride at least fifty times before.

As they rode, Clint and Zeke didn't talk very much. What few words they did say to one another were almost lost amid the pounding of their horses' hooves against the ground. Every so often, Zeke would point in a direction away from the beaten path and then steer his horse that way. Clint learned early on to follow the other man quickly, or he would risk losing Zeke altogether.

Zeke's shortcuts branched from the main path that fed back into another path. In between, there was some rugged terrain that was overgrown with tall grass, trees and rocks.

Some of it was also coated with thick layers of frost or just enough ice to threaten even Eclipse's footing along the way.

Clint wasn't even able to see many of the shortcuts that Zeke was heading toward until after he broke through and rode onto them. Even then, a few of the paths were still almost invisible to the naked eye. All Clint could do was follow in Zeke's footsteps until some of the ground cleared up beneath him.

All the while, Clint was plotting their course on a map in his head. Shortcuts like these weren't shown to him every day. They would certainly come in handy some other time when he came through this area, and they were definitely a big help now.

They had to make camp just once, and that was only for a few hours to eat, rest the horses and catch a bit of sleep for themselves. They made it to Ambling Creek at sundown, and every one of them, both horses included, were almost too tired to take another step.

"Oh my God," Zeke whispered once they rode onto the main street cutting through the middle of Ambling Creek.

It had been a while since Clint had been there, but the empty buildings and deserted streets were pretty much as he remembered. For Zeke, however, the sight was anything but familiar. In fact, the look on his face made it seem as though he was looking straight into the eyes of a ghost.

The sun was just a sliver on the horizon, but was more than enough to show Clint the horror on Zeke's face. His mouth hung open as he kept trying to speak. No words came out, however, and his eyes kept darting back and forth to take everything in.

"When was the last time you were here?" Clint asked.

". . . Eight months. Maybe ten."

"And what was it like?"

It took a moment, but Zeke finally responded, "Alive. This place was alive when I was here last time. Now, it's . . ." His voice trailed off as though it had just run out of steam. The man simply didn't have the strength to utter the last word in his sentence.

"Where does your uncle live?" Clint asked.

That question was like a splash of cold water in Zeke's face. "Oh God. This way." Without looking to see if Clint was following, Zeke snapped his reins and raced down the empty street.

Having become used to trailing in Zeke's steps, Clint was right behind him as the man took him to a row of houses clustered on the other side of town. As he rode, Clint recalled what he'd seen the previous time he'd been to the town.

As before, the main thing he saw was that there simply wasn't anything to see. It was the common factor for any ghost town: desolation.

Unlike the first time, however, Clint looked a bit closer at the buildings he passed. He wasn't satisfied with the idea that they were just empty. He'd come all this way to see if he could piece together how the town had been emptied. Learning that would go a long way in telling him what to expect when the Reapers came to the Double Briar in force.

But as much as he tried, Clint simply couldn't get a very good look at the town while passing through it. Part of that was because he was rushing to keep up with Zeke. Another part of the problem was that his own eyes were tired and their lids were drooping lower with every passing second.

It wasn't a long ride from one end of Ambling Creek to the other. But without so much as a single person on the street or even the sound of a single voice along the way, that ride seemed a hell of a lot longer.

THIRTY-ONE

Zeke stood on the porch of a house that looked like it was about to collapse in on itself. He reached out to touch one of the posts supporting the front awning, but pulled his hand back before making contact. The look on his face had darkened the closer he got to this spot. When he turned to look at Clint, his expression was almost lifeless.

"They're gone," Zeke said in a voice that was almost too quiet to be heard over the breeze. "All of them. Every last one."

Clint stepped forward, being careful not to go any farther than Zeke, himself, had gone. "How many lived here?"

"My uncle and his kids. There were four of them last time I was here to visit, but there could have been more. He took in folks from time to time if they had nowhere else to go. Sometimes family came here to stay for a spell before moving on. Usually they was heading west."

Clint looked at the front of the house. He noticed that the door was ajar and he started to step toward it. Before touching the handle, he looked back to Zeke.

The other man nodded to answer the unspoken question in Clint's eyes. In fact, he seemed relieved that Clint was going to take the first step into the house.

All it took was a tap of Clint's hand to send the door swinging open. The hinges creaked loudly, sending an echo into the rest of the house which almost sounded like a scream. Stepping into the house, Clint's hand reflexively drifted toward the Colt at his side.

"Hello?" he shouted into the home. Even as he shouted a few more words into the darkness, Clint knew he wasn't going to get an answer. The air was too still to hold a reply. Even if someone was hiding, they couldn't keep that quiet.

The house was filled with the winter's chill. It felt more like a cave than a home. The cold had seeped into every inch without once being chased away by a fire or the warmth of life.

Zeke's footsteps echoed loudly behind Clint's. Once he was inside, Zeke shook off the sluggishness that had hindered him on the other side of the threshold. "Uncle Carl?" he shouted while jogging through each room of the house. "Ginny? Anyone?"

As Zeke raced through the house, calling out to relatives who weren't there, Clint took a little more time to examine the place. He couldn't see much, due to the fading light coming in from the outside. When he tried to find a lantern, all he got was broken glass and dented tin. With the light fading quickly, Clint reached into a pocket and found a match. There was no shortage of rough surfaces to strike it upon.

The little flame came to life and filled the small room with a flickering glow. Clint hoped to be able to see well enough to find something in one of the piles on the floor, but he had no such luck. It wasn't so much that there wasn't enough light. It was simply that there wasn't anything he could use.

The room where Clint stood looked as though it might have been a study. It could have also been a sitting room, but it was hard to tell which due to the mess that covered almost every inch of the floor. Piles of broken shelves lay against the walls, with ripped books scattered among them.

Tattered rugs, splintered chairs, even smashed furniture could be found with a single glance. The rest of what Clint could see was broken almost beyond recognition.

When he turned back toward the entryway, Clint found Zeke standing there with his arms hanging at his sides. The last bit of light from Clint's match glinted off the gun clutched in Zeke's hand.

"You find anything, Zeke?"

The black man was too stunned to answer right away. Before Clint repeated his question, Zeke managed to blink a few times and look directly at him. "Just a bunch of junk. Just enough for me to know that Uncle Carl and the rest were here. Other than that . . . nothing."

"What about a lantern?" Clint asked, trying to keep his voice calm and his questions simple. "We could use some light."

Although he was still rattled, Zeke managed to respond with a shake of his head. "There's nothing, Clint. Everything that was here is busted to pieces, ripped up or cracked open."

Before he wasted another match, Clint reached down to one of the piles in the room he'd just left. Half a table lay amid a heap of overturned drawers. Clint set his foot against the table and pulled off one of the legs that clung to it by a nail and a half.

Zeke looked over at Clint with angry eyes, but he quickly saw that there wasn't anything more Clint could do to make his uncle's house any worse.

Bypassing the more recognizable remains of carpeting, Clint found some curtains, tore off a few strips and wrapped them around the end of the table leg. He then took out a match, struck it and touched the flame to the tattered material. The curtain material ignited before too long and filled the room with more than enough light to see.

Zeke followed the same procedure and touched the end of his own makeshift torch to Clint's. Now both men could get a better look around.

"This place was ransacked," Clint pointed out. "Looks like a bunch of men went through here and just smashed everything they could. Did your uncle have any valuables?"

"Not much. Let me check." With that, Zeke made his way to one of the rooms upstairs. He came back down to the sitting room, shaking his head. "Uncle Carl had a bit of money stashed and some jewelry. Nothing big. Just my granny's rings. They're all gone, though."

Clint spotted some bullet holes toward the back of the room, but didn't mention them to Zeke just then. The man already looked as though he'd been kicked in the stomach. Still, there was one question he needed to ask. "Did you find . . . any of them?"

"No. Apart from us, there ain't no one here. Dead or alive."

"We need to get a look at the rest of the town."

"What for? There isn't nothing here!"

"There's plenty here," Clint replied, still keeping his voice measured and calm. "That's why we came. Let's check as many of the nearby houses and shops that we can. After we get some sleep, we can walk the rest of the town and see what we can see. We can sleep here if you like."

Zeke was already heading out the front door. "No. I don't want to step foot in this place again."

THIRTY-TWO

That night passed without more than a few words passing between Clint and Zeke. Both men felt the weight of their ride pressing down on them harder with every extra minute they kept their eyes open. They walked the streets of Ambling Creek, surveying the damage that had essentially cleared out the whole town.

As far as Clint could tell, no part of the town hadn't been put to the torch. Then again, that wouldn't have caused any more damage than what had been done. The night was spent mostly combing through the place, looking for signs of life. Once that was done, both men looked for a spot to collapse.

The horses had found a fair amount of shelter in the stables, which turned out to be one of the buildings with the least amount of damage. By the time Clint and Zeke were through with their walk, they'd both come to the same conclusion.

Eclipse and Zeke's horse were in separate stalls toward the back of the stable. Clint and Zeke, themselves, had picked out their own stalls closer to the front of the large building. After spending the last few hours walking through the bleak remains of Ambling Creek, spending the night in the stable didn't seem like too bad of an idea.

There were no widows to break and hardly any furniture to destroy. In fact, apart from a few bullet holes in the walls, the stable was in fairly good condition. One thing was for certain. Sleeping there beat the hell out of spending any more time in a room occupied only by ghosts.

Clint's bedroll was spread out on a mattress of loose straw. A fire was going in the middle of the drafty stable, crackling at the bottom of a shallow pit that had been dug into the floor. He sat with his back against the wall in a spot where he could see both ends of the building as well as most of the loft over his head.

"You know something?" Clint asked while glancing across to the stall where Zeke was stretching out. "This isn't half bad."

The darkness that had been on Zeke's face since seeing his uncle's house was still there. When he heard Clint's statement and then took a look for himself, however, he couldn't help but smile. "You're right. I never thought laying in a bunch of hay would feel so good."

"Just try not to think about where that hay's been."

Zeke winced and then broke out in laughter. Clint joined him as well, allowing himself to relax a little after a very long day. Once they were finished, they were even more tired. Tired and hungry.

Clint opened his eyes and wondered if he would ever get to sleep. When he tried to move, every one of his joints begged for mercy. The next thing he noticed was that there was no longer any light coming from the middle of the room.

The wind brushed against the outside of the stable, rattling boards and pushing around leaves on the roof. Clint sat up and stretched his arms, noticing that the fire was completely out. There wasn't much more than a veil of smoke hanging over the pit.

Pulling the watch from his pocket, Clint saw that it was actually getting close to dawn. Although it hadn't been the best of his life, he had managed to get a few hours of sleep. Of course, that didn't do much for the rumbling in his belly. He went to his saddlebags, gathered some cooking supplies and started collecting more wood to be piled in the pit.

Zeke joined him soon, and the two quickly put together a simple breakfast which was downed without taking the time to enjoy it. There was plenty more to do, and both men could feel their time was growing short.

"Do you think Mr. Ossutt's holding out all right?" Zeke asked, voicing the same question that had been on Clint's mind.

"I hope so." He tore off a chunk of bacon and chewed it before nodding. "He should be all right. At least, he should be able to strike a deal that'll buy him some more time."

"Doesn't look to me like the men that did this are the kind to strike a deal."

Clint knew that Hank Ossutt had already had words with the leader of the Reapers. He also knew that, more than likely, that same outlaw leader would approach him one more time to see if Ossutt would be willing to buy his way out of this mess.

Although Will Dreyer probably would take whatever money was offered and tear down the Double Briar anyway, the process would take some time. Clint just had to hope that it would be enough time for him and Zeke to return with whatever knowledge they'd acquired.

But telling all of this to Zeke might not be a good idea. Clint realized that when he thought back to the look that had been on Zeke's face at his uncle's house. Knowing that Ossutt had exchanged words with Dreyer might be enough to push the man over the edge.

On the other hand, Zeke might already know that Dreyer had been to see Ossutt. Either way, it didn't make much sense to bring it up now.

"What the hell are we gonna do, Clint?" Zeke asked after tossing out the rest of his coffee.

"Just what we came here to do. Get a look at this place and see if we can figure out how these outlaws work."

"I mean after that. Even if we do learn something, what do we do with it? Take all those men on? Hell, even the law won't do that."

"Really?"

Zeke nodded. "Me and some others went into Flat Rock to talk to the sheriff there. He said there wasn't nothing to do unless he got together a posse." Shaking his head, he added, "I don't even think he tried."

"Well, there goes my backup plan. I guess we won't be making that stop along the way back, after all."

"So where does that leave us?"

"It leaves us with plenty of work to do and not enough time to do it." With that, Clint got up and headed out of the stable.

Zeke was right behind him.

Once they were outside, Clint went left and Zeke went right. They looked through the town in a few hours and were out before noon. Clint only hoped they could get back in time to put what he'd learned to use. Even if they did, he figured their odds still weren't all that good.

THIRTY-THREE

The last few days had gone by slowly for everyone at the Double Briar. For Hank Ossutt, however, they seemed to melt into one long stream of minutes, each of them more taxing than the one before it. His eyes were surrounded by dark circles and his face seemed to be hanging off the front of his skull.

"Any word from Adams yet?" Hank asked one of the ranch hands sitting at the dining table.

The younger man shook his head and got back to the soup he was eating.

"He'll be back," came a familiar, booming voice from the little hospital that had been set up at the back of the house. Mace walked with a limp and was tucking his shirt in gently over the bandaged wound on his side. "Say what you want about that one, but The Gunsmith isn't the type to cut and run."

"What are you doing here?" Hank asked wearily.

Mace waved off the question and kept walking until he was close enough to look out one of the windows. "You've had me doing the light work around here as if I lost an arm. You and Kyle still need me to wipe yer noses just like always."

Hank smirked at that. "Good point."

"Then what needs doing? I mean, besides the chores you've had me running lately."

"Are you sure you're feeling up to it?" Hank asked.

"All I needed was a little rest and some bandages. I could've been back at my duties the next day, but you've been too pigheaded to see that. And the rest of these boys are too scared of you to ride out with me unless you say so."

Hank looked around at the few other ranch hands in sight. Sure enough, most of them either winced or looked away completely rather than meet his gaze head-on. "I don't want anyone else to get hurt. That's all."

"Oh, is that all?" Stepping forward, Mace made sure he was close enough to speak to Hank without being over-heard before continuing. "Is that why you're too distracted to keep an eye on your own daughter?"

"Lynne? What's she got to do with anything?"

"Not much. But you might be interested in the company she's been keeping behind your back."

"What are you talking about?" Hank asked as his eyes narrowed into angry slits. "Who's with my daughter?"

"I don't know for certain, but there's definitely someone sneaking around up there. I've heard it from that damn bed you make me sleep in in the house."

Hank's hand drifted toward the gun at his side. "Is he still up there?"

"No. Someone snuck out after she came down for breakfast this morning. Real quiet, but I heard them steps. Real quick, too, because they were gone before I could track them down. I did get a look at him jumping the fence and heading south."

"On foot?"

Mace nodded.

"Then go find him."

"Say no more," Mace said. "I'll get some boys together and we'll take a ride. Let's start with you," he said, slap-

ping the back of the young man who'd been working on his
bowl of soup.

Mace's hand clapped so hard against the other man's
back that soup splashed from his bowl as well as from the
spoon in his hand to splatter all over the front of his shirt.

The soup eater looked more disappointed that his meal
was getting cut short than he was upset about the mess. In
a grumbling voice, he said, "But I just sat down to—"

"That's the spirit!" Mace boomed. "Now get yer coat
and follow me."

The younger man followed Mace out the door. By the
look on his face, he was well aware that he had no other
choice in the matter.

Hank watched them go, following to stand in the open
doorway leading out to the front of the house. Shortly, his
eyes found something else of interest in the vicinity of the
front gate surrounding the house. At first, he thought the
two riders were Clint and Zeke returning from their ride to
Ambling Creek. A few seconds later, he knew that wasn't
the case.

Hank's first instinct was to run.

He knew better than to think he could get away. In fact,
getting away wasn't even the desire behind his reflex. He
wanted to run into the house to get the rifle that he'd left
propped behind the desk in his study. There was a pistol at
his side, but the rancher wasn't foolish enough to think that
he could use that weapon well enough to warrant clearing
leather.

By the time those two riders got into pistol range, they
would be close enough to gun him down themselves. Will
Dreyer was just crazy enough to try something like that.

THIRTY-FOUR

With all the armed men coming and going through the front gates of the ranch house, most of the men on the property didn't notice two more. Most of those who did notice didn't look closely enough at their faces to remember them a few seconds later. Those few who did look didn't recognize Will Dreyer as the very man who'd stirred up all the commotion in the first place.

Will rode through the men, smiling wider as he got closer and closer to the house. When he spotted Hank Ossutt standing on the front porch, that smile became wide enough to see from a mile away.

"He's going for his gun," the man riding next to Will warned.

Will shook his head without taking his eyes from the rancher. "He won't draw it. He's too scared."

Although the man riding next to Will had his doubts, he kept from doing anything about them. His hand settled over the grip of his gun and stayed there. Much to his surprise, Will's prediction was right. Hank didn't draw, although the look in his eyes showed that he sure as hell wanted to.

"What the hell are you doing on my property?" Hank snarled.

A few of the others in the area glanced back to see who the rancher was talking to. That was all it took for them to get a taste of the tension that crackled between Ossutt and the other two riders. Slowly, a few of the ranch hands drifted closer to the house.

Will shrugged and leaned casually in his saddle. "Just passing through. I'd like to have a word with you somewhere out of the cold."

"We can talk fine right here."

"Come on now, Hank. Where's your hospitality?"

"Ain't none for you."

"Now if you decide to talk rudely, then I'll have to do the same. Do you really want to start something like that?"

One of the rancher's men stepped onto the porch and stood next to Ossutt. "You need some help, Hank?"

Inside his head, Hank was screaming for help. He was begging for one or all of his men to draw guns and open fire on the two smug bastards in front of him. But he knew that would only cause Dreyer and his partner to open fire as well.

He also knew that the Reapers were a hell of a lot better in a gun battle. Some might say that such a thing was the very element they thrived in.

"It's all right," Hank said to the younger man next to him.

"You gonna offer me a drink?" Dreyer asked.

The self-satisfied tone in Dreyer's voice was meant to dig under Ossutt's skin. Not only did it succeed, but it succeeded so well that Hank almost went for his own gun and forgot about the hell that might unleash.

"We'll talk right here," Hank said. "Say what you mean to say and get off my land."

That caught the attention of every armed ranch hand in the area. Although some of them had already ridden out of earshot, at least half a dozen of them stepped up to form a rough circle around the two riders.

Although he saw what was happening around him, Dreyer didn't seem concerned by it in the least. "You're holding one of my men," Dreyer said, cutting straight to the heart of the matter. "You're not the law and you don't got the right to hold anyone against their will."

The younger man at Ossutt's side bristled. "Is this the son of a bitch we're after?"

"Matt, don't," Hank said, reaching out to put a hand on the younger man's arm. But it was too late for him to get ahold of Matt's wrist before he went for his gun.

The ranch hand got a grip on his pistol and started to pull it from its holster. That was as far as he got before the rider accompanying Dreyer cleared leather and took aim at Matt.

"Everyone stand still!" Hank shouted to the men around him as they started grabbing for their own weapons.

All of the ranch hands heard the order come from Hank's mouth. A few of them, however, didn't look too happy about it.

Will nodded as he smiled and looked around at the armed men surrounding him. "You've got a good bunch of boys here, Hank. It seems like you're interested in keeping them alive. That's good."

"If you're after your man, you're out of luck," Hank said. "You're so interested in the law? Then you go get the law and bring them here. I'm sure they'll love to hear about the threats you've made and the men of mine that you've shot."

"I haven't shot any of your men," Will replied in a tone that actually sounded offended. "And neither has my associate here."

"Maybe not that one, but some of your boys sure as hell did. Since you already admit that the man I've got is one of yours, then that means the rest of them were, too. Those men did their best to kill my boys."

"I guess you've got me there."

"You're damn right I do. And if you try to harm me, my family or anyone who works for me, I'll make you sorry you even set foot on the Double Briar."

The smile hung on Dreyer's face, but it now seemed more like something that had been painted onto a corpse. His eyes became cold and deadly. Even some of the color seemed to drain from his skin. "Is that a threat?"

Hank didn't reply. He kept his chin up and his back straight for the sake of his workers, but inside he was shaking like a leaf.

"I gave you a chance to be done with this, but you decided to play it out," Dreyer said. "You don't want to force my play, old man, because I've got enough firepower to bring this whole filthy place to the ground! The only reason any of your men are still alive is because of me.

"I gave you a deadline and I aim to keep it. But your time's running out and my men are getting real anxious to come in here and take what you got." Leaning forward in his saddle, Dreyer spoke as if he and Hank were the only two people in the world. "I've heard that daughter of yours is a real sweet one. I bet she wouldn't even mind fucking my men two at a time. I guess we'll find out soon enough."

The man with Dreyer still had his gun drawn. By now, he'd managed to get his other hand wrapped around a pistol as well and was aiming it at another group of ranch hands. His face had become like stone and he already seemed resolved to the fact that blood was about to be spilled. The only question he had was which rancher to kill first.

Hank's face reddened and his hands clenched into fists. All the men around him were looking at him, waiting for the order to fire. Even a twitch in the right direction would have been good enough for them to pull their triggers.

Finally, Hank's mouth opened just enough for a snarling voice to come out. "Get . . . off . . . my . . . property."

"One day," Dreyer said while holding up a single finger that stabbed straight up to the sky. "That's all you got before you see me again. It's up to you whether or not I'm the last face you see before you meet your maker."

With that, Dreyer steered his horse toward the gate and took off. The man accompanying him kept his sights on the ranchers for a while before following Dreyer through the gate.

THIRTY-FIVE

"Are you gonna let them go?" Matt asked. "After what they did? After what they said?"

"Shut up, Matt," Hank snapped. Before the younger man could respond, Hank pointed toward the fence.

A figure stood up and made itself known for a brief instant. Another silhouette followed a little farther along the fence. Then there was another and another after that. Each of the silhouettes were that of a man carrying a rifle.

"They wanted us to fire on them," Hank said in a defeated tone. "They were just waiting for the order to shoot."

Matt looked around at the riflemen in the distance as the figures faded away. "If now's not the time to do something, then when is? We can't just wait around for them to come back!"

Hank was already on his way back into the house. "I know, Matt. I know."

Before Hank got through the door, Matt was grabbing him by the elbow and pulling him back out. "That's not good enough! There's more than just you and yours here, Mr. Ossutt. You've got a whole crew of men putting their lives on the line for you.

"I know you've done plenty for your men and we all ap-

preciate it. Hell, we strapped on our guns and rode on patrol when two ambushes had already happened right here
at the Double Briar. Why the hell do you want us heeled
and guarding this place if you won't let us do something
when a killer walks right up to the front porch and has a
word with you?"

Hank looked around and saw that all of his men were
looking right back at him expectantly.

"We want to stand by you," Matt continued. "But not if
we're just supposed to do nothing and wait to be killed in
another ambush."

Although he'd been angered by the younger man's tone
at first, Hank now saw the truth in his words. More than
that, he saw the same sentiments reflected on all the other
faces gathered around the front of the house.

"You're good men," Hank said. "All of you. But this
wasn't just that bastard riding up to have a chat. This was
an ambush waiting to happen. And if anyone had stepped
out of line a few moments ago, it would have become a
slaughter."

"Be that as it may, we're either going to do something
about them killers or we're letting you face them on your
own." There was some regret in Matt's eyes when he said
that, but there was also a fair amount of determination.

"I don't want to get you men killed," Hank said. "And
since we've got to take care of our own, I don't intend on
letting that piece of trash have his way."

"So what are we going to do?"

The question was simple, but the answer was the very
thing that had been sitting in Hank's gut like a pit for too
long. As much as he didn't want to lie to his men, he also
didn't want them to know just how desperate the situation
truly was.

Then again, the rancher had batted around the idea of
telling them all just that. If they wanted to stay, they would

stay. If they wanted to leave, then he truly couldn't blame them.

Seeing the growing anxiousness in Matt's face, Hank pulled in a breath and said, "You men should prob—"

"Mr. Ossutt!" a man shouted as he rode around from behind the house. "Mr. Ossutt, someone's coming!"

The rancher tensed, along with all of the armed workers. The ranch hands lifted their guns, eager to have a target to replace the one that had ridden away without a care in the world. Even Hank looked ready to fire. In his mind, the notion of stepping into an ambush was looking better than waiting around for it.

"Who's coming?" Hank asked. "Did you get a look at them?"

"There's just one of them," the man said breathlessly. "And he's headed straight for us."

"Someone bring me a horse." That was all Hank had to say to get practically every man around him into motion.

Matt and the rest of the ranch hands scattered to either get their own horses from where they were hitched or to head off in the direction from which the other rider had come. Hank didn't even get a look at who'd brought his horse around. All he did was take the reins and climb into the saddle.

"Nobody fire until I say so," Hank shouted to the others as he rode by them.

Some of the ranch hands looked over to Matt and got a nod of approval from the young man.

Hank saw this subtle challenge to his authority, but ignored it for the moment. There were bigger concerns to be dealt with for now.

By the time he got around his house, Hank had a posse of four men carrying guns who were plenty eager to use them. He spotted the rider approaching the fence and spurred his horse to meet him head-on. Hank's hand tightened around his pistol and his eyes focused on the solitary rider in his sights.

"Hold up!" Hank said. "It's Zeke."

Before any of the others could bring their horses to a stop, Hank turned to them and shouted, "You men get back on patrol. I don't want anyone else to be able to slip through here like them other two! Move it!"

With that kind of fire in his voice, Hank was able to get the ranch hands moving before they had a chance to check in with Matt. For his part, Matt seemed pleased by that and he stayed at Ossutt's side to wait for Zeke to approach.

"Where's Clint?" Hank asked as soon as Zeke was close enough to hear him.

Zeke was already shaking his head as he brought his horse to a stop. "He's gone, Hank. He didn't make it."

"What?" Matt was stunned.

Hank felt as if he'd just gotten booted in the gut and then stomped into the dirt. He'd never really considered the possibility of losing his ranch or seeing his family killed.

Not until that moment.

THIRTY-SIX

Andy lay in the weeds just on the other side of the fence. He'd been laying there for a few hours without allowing himself to move from the spot. It was the perfect place to see and hear most of what went on in front of the ranch house, which was the main spot where people came and went. Even Hank Ossutt himself stood out on that porch and gave orders to his men.

But doing his job wasn't foremost on his mind. Just ahead of that was the knowledge that Will Dreyer would put a bullet through Andy's head, quick as you please, if he budged without anything to show for it. This was something, all right. This was something big.

Crawling through the overgrowth, Andy wriggled like a snake until he was far enough away to risk getting onto his feet. Even then, he kept his knees bent so he was half his height until he got to the spot where his horse was tied.

It was a spot where plenty of the ranch hands tied their horses. Now with so many men coming and going, one more animal in the pack was easy enough to overlook. Andy picked his moment when no other riders were about, climbed into his saddle and rode off.

He cleared the property line at a spot where the fence

hung a bit lower due to a few rotted rails. In truth, he could
have ridden that path with his eyes closed. Andy had been
scouting for it and other blind spots on the property ever
since Will Dreyer made his first visit.

That was how Andy had been able to slip away so con-
vincingly when his moment came. That was how he managed to stay hidden despite all the men riding the property.
That was even how he managed to pay Lynne a visit every
now and then.

Andy split off from his intended path just after clearing
Ossutt's property. He needed to check in on one other matter, but that only took a few minutes. After that, he was free
to head straight to where Dreyer was waiting.

Going by the look on the outlaw's face, Dreyer wasn't
too fond of waiting.

"What took you so long?" Dreyer asked.

Andy brought his horse up next to Dreyer's. Even
though both men were in their saddles, the outlaw still
seemed to look down as though Andy was still crawling on
his belly.

"I had to take a roundabout way to get here," Andy
replied.

"Did anyone see you?"

"Hell no. They was stirred up like a bunch of wild
turkeys after you left. I doubt they were even thinking
straight."

"Did Ossutt send men after us?"

"Not directly. He sent out some more men, but he's still
holding off."

More to himself, Dreyer asked, "What's he waiting
for?"

"Adams," Andy replied.

"Adams? None of us have seen him for days."

"He must've slipped out to go do something or other for
Hank. Hell if I know how he got past us."

Dreyer's eyes narrowed and he looked down at Andy

with no small amount of contempt. "How did you know Adams was still here? Did you see him?"

"No, but I did hear something you'll like."

"What is it?" Dreyer demanded. He was already getting tired of the conversation.

"That black fellow came riding up not too long after you and Beeman left. I guess he was riding with Adams before. Anyway, he says that Clint Adams didn't make it."

Dreyer's eyes snapped over to the members of his gang that were nearby. Each one of them gave a subtle shake of his head or a shrug in response to the question in Dreyer's glare.

Andy looked so happy with himself that he might burst. "Either he did cut and run or one of your men got him without realizing who they shot. Hell, someone else might've caught him with a lucky shot. Who cares? Gone is gone! Isn't that great news?"

Although Andy was all smiles, the rest of the men didn't seem so happy. When he looked around for approval, all Andy got was a few unimpressed grunts. The only real noise following his report came from the horses.

"Yeah, Andy," Dreyer said before the younger man started up again. "That's great. Why don't you head back and find someplace to lay low for a while. Check back here this time tomorrow."

"Tomorrow? Oh . . . well, okay. I'll see you guys tomorrow."

Andy trotted away from the group and headed back toward the house.

A few seconds later, Dreyer let out the sigh he'd been choking on the entire time Andy had been there.

Beeman, the gunman who'd been with Dreyer on his last visit to Hank's house, brought his horse a little closer. "You think he's telling the truth?"

"I don't think he's lying," Dreyer replied. "But that still don't make what he heard the truth. Having Adams disap-

pear right now is too much of a good thing. He's probably
sneaking around here somewhere. This is a big ranch and
if that dumb shit Andy can sneak around it, than a man like
Clint Adams shouldn't have any problem."

"What about what he overheard? What do you think
about that?"

"I'll believe it when I see Adams's body. If it's true, than
we shouldn't have any trouble when we ride in and tear that
place down later tonight. If it's not, than Andy took bad in-
formation for gospel. Either way, he's not much use to us
anymore."

Snapping his fingers at one of the other men nearby,
Dreyer said to him, "Follow Andy to wherever he's going.
If you lose him, you should be able to pick him up again
when he goes back to fuck that rancher's daughter like he
was always bragging about. He thinks he's got until tomorrow, so he'll have his guard down for a while."

The gunman nodded with a very genuine smile.

"When you find him," Dreyer added, "kill him. But keep
the body hidden. Maybe that rancher will hand over some
more if he thinks he can save the kid's life. At least that
might save us some time in looking through all the rubble
for some bunch of money that was hid away."

"I don't mind looking," Beeman said.

"I know you don't, but there's always some wad of
money under a floorboard that we could miss. Not this
time. This rancher's like a gold mine, stuck out here all on
his own without the law anywhere close. I don't want to
miss a thing."

The other gunman had snapped his reins and gone rid-
ing off on a path that would circle around and catch up to
Andy. Another man stepped up to take his place around
Dreyer, followed by another and another.

"What about Adams?" Beeman asked. "I get the feeling
he's still alive somewhere."

"If he is, he'll show himself. There's no use in stopping

what we're doing just to split up and look for him. If he's dead, that suits me just fine."

Beeman waited for a moment before asking, "You don't really believe he's dead, do you?"

After a while, Dreyer shook his head. "Nah. He could be somewhere around here and we'll deal with him if he is. But odds are better he just headed for greener pastures. If he had a brain in his head, he's in a saloon somewhere toasting the fact that he ain't here no more. Once we're done with this place, the only ones who'll want to be here are the buzzards."

THIRTY-SEVEN

More than anything, Andy wanted to ride back to the house and climb up into Lynne's bed. It looked like he would have plenty of time until Dreyer needed him, so that left some room for him to play. The only thing that kept him from doing just that was the part of his brain that wasn't centered in his groin.

After Dreyer's visit, the ranch hands were itching for a fight and were swarming all over the property. Although he was fairly confident that he could stay clear of them, Andy knew that Dreyer wouldn't like it too much if he was found.

That still left Andy with someplace to go. The cabin wasn't much more than four rickety walls leaning together. The smokehouse where Nick was being held was actually roomy compared to this place. Even so, that cabin would have to do until it got a bit darker.

Stuck out in the middle of nowhere less than a quarter mile from the Double Briar, Andy's cabin was practically invisible to anyone riding by on the rundown trail skirting Flat Rock. Even if someone did spot it, they might easily mistake the cabin for a mess of old lumber or even a huge, rotted out tree stump.

But Andy knew better. He also knew that, considering who was waiting for him in that cabin, there was no reason for him to do a little playing.

"Hello, darlin'," Andy said as he walked up to the cabin and pulled open the door. "I'm back."

Inside, there was just a stool, some supplies scattered on the floor and a post in the middle of the room which held the cabin up. Tied to that post, more angry than scared, was a blonde who was very much out of her element.

"Didn't think you'd see me so soon, did you, Percy?" Andy asked as he stepped into the cabin and pulled the door shut behind him. As he sat down on the stool, he eyed the blonde with hungry desire.

Phoebe didn't even try to speak through the knotted bandanna wrapped over her mouth.

"I know I said I wouldn't be back for a while, but that's changed. I got some time on my hands and that means that I get to sit and have a little fun with you for a while."

Looking at the grinning young man, Phoebe thought back yet again to the rush of events that led to her being tied to that spot. No matter how many times she went over it, she couldn't pick out more than a few details.

The memories started when she'd opened the door to Lynne's room for a chance to get in and clean while the rancher's daughter was out. Phoebe had had her suspicions that Lynne was meeting up with one of the ranch hands. She even thought that it could have been a few ranch hands. What she hadn't expected was to find Andy in that room hopping into his boots.

At first, she'd been happy to see the man that everyone had feared was hurt or dead. But when she got a look at the fire in Andy's eyes, Phoebe knew that there was something else going on.

Andy hadn't been hurt. He certainly wasn't dead and he didn't much like the fact that he'd been discovered.

Just as she'd realized that she might be in trouble,

Phoebe saw Andy jump at her. His fist lashed out and there was a knock to her face, followed by a throbbing pain that filled her head even now.

She recalled falling, but not hitting the ground. She left the house, but not on her own, and when she woke up, her hands were being tied to a post.

The fog had just cleared from her head when she saw Andy pointing a gun at her. But the young man couldn't get himself to pull the trigger. He'd gagged her and then stomped out. All of that had to have happened in the last several hours, although it felt to her like it had been a whole lot longer than that.

Andy was sitting on the stool, leering at her as if she was the first woman he'd ever seen. "You're pretty," he whispered.

She turned her eyes away, hoping that that didn't just make him more interested in her. Phoebe pulled against the post that kept her staked to the ground, even though she'd already wasted plenty of strength trying to get free while Andy had been away.

Eventually, like the inevitable shots from a firing squad, Phoebe felt Andy's hand press against her skin. He was pulling at her blouse, fumbling to get a feel beneath it. Finally, she felt his hand on her bare skin, palming her firm breast, pinching her nipple.

"Mmm, that's nice," he grunted, huskily. "Let's play."

Phoebe clenched her eyes shut and tried to think about anything other than where she was and what was about to happen. She did her best to kick and struggle against him, but there was only so much she could do from her vulnerable position on the ground.

And just as he got both hands inside her dress, when she was about to resign herself to the unthinkable, Phoebe's last, desperate prayer was answered.

A sound exploded through the cabin, filling every inch of air with a thunderous roar. Each of the four walls rattled, shaking dust and splinters down onto Andy and Phoebe's heads.

Her eyes opened to get a look at what was happening, but all she could see was Andy's face pressed right up against her. His eyes were still shut and his mouth was curved into a sloppy smile. His hands still groped for Phoebe's breasts, even when the door was knocked in after the second thundering impact.

Although she couldn't see much past Andy, Phoebe was able to catch a glimpse of the hand that slammed down onto Andy's shoulder and pulled him back. Another hand followed the first, only this one was balled into a meaty fist.

The impact of the punch took Andy completely out of Phoebe's sight, giving her a clear view of the one who'd stormed into the cabin.

THIRTY-EIGHT

"Oh my God," Phoebe gasped as soon as the bandanna was pulled away from her mouth. "Clint, is that really you?"

Rather that untie the rope securing Phoebe to the post, Clint used his pocketknife to cut straight through it. "It's me, all right. My question is what the hell you're doing here."

"Andy knocked me out and dragged me here when I found him in the house. He was with Lynne, that dirty whore."

"I figured there might be someone close to Ossutt working for the Reapers."

"The Reapers?"

"It's a long story." Clint took Phoebe's hand and helped her to her feet. "But now's not the time for me to tell it. I need to get you out of here."

"How'd you find me?"

"I split off to get some scouting done on my own. Some of the gunmen paid Hank a visit and Andy here was sneaking away after they left. I followed him to where the others were and then caught up with him here. When I heard him talking to someone, it didn't sound friendly so I stepped in. Hope I wasn't too late."

Phoebe's hands were free and the bandanna was finally

152

off her face completely. Rather than say anything to Clint, she reached out and took hold of his face in both of her hands. She then leaned in to give him a kiss that was every bit as fiery as Clint's entrance only moments ago.

"You were just in time," she said with a grateful smile.

Unfortunately, that smile lasted for all of another two seconds before Phoebe's eyes widened and her voice lifted in a surprised scream.

"Clint, look out!"

Still reeling a bit from the kiss that Phoebe had planted on him, Clint was just a little slow in reacting to the rustling sounds he'd been hearing. By the time he knew that Andy was getting back to his feet, Phoebe was too close for him to do much of anything more than push her toward the other side of the room.

Clint pivoted to get a look at what Andy was doing, and was just in time for the side of his face to meet the other man's fist. Although it was a painful meeting, it was better than if Andy had been able to knock Clint in the back of his head.

Andy's fist glanced off of Clint's jaw and Clint did his best to roll with the impact. By the looks of it, it seemed that Andy almost knocked Clint off his feet. In fact, that's exactly what Andy thought he'd done.

"That's right, Adams!" Andy snarled victoriously. "You're not so bad!"

Clint had allowed himself to be twisted around and almost brought down to one knee. For him, that was a way to take the edge off the punch while also getting him in a good spot to strike back. That answer came in no time at all as Clint pulled himself back around and took a swing that practically started down at the cabin's dirty floor.

Andy was still smiling when Clint's fist swept upward like a cracking whip. The punch landed directly under Andy's chin, making a noise very similar to that same whip. The snap of knuckles against jaw sent Andy's head straight back while also lifting him partially off the ground.

Blood sprayed through the air, jetting from Andy's lip to make a red streak on the wall. Andy reached out with both hands, searching reflexively for something to steady himself. He came up empty as his back slammed against the wall and he slumped to the floor.

"Phoebe, get out of here," Clint ordered.

The blonde heard her name and instantly moved to do as Clint asked. She hopped around Andy's flailing legs and headed straight for the door which still wobbled upon its rusty hinges.

Turning to make sure that she got out all right, Clint spotted something else outside the cabin. It wasn't much more than a blur of movement, but it was plenty to get him moving even faster. Rather than shout another order to Phoebe, Clint reached out with one hand while taking a lunging step forward.

The palm of Clint's hand pressed against the top of Phoebe's head, forcing her down roughly. His other hand was wrapped around the modified Colt, which he quickly aimed and fired through the newly vacated space.

The figure Clint had spotted dove for cover, just in time to keep from getting hit by that first shot.

Moving his left hand down from Phoebe's head to her shoulder, Clint pulled her back into the cabin. "Did Andy have anyone else over here?"

"No," she replied. "Not while I was here."

"Then maybe these are some of Hank's boys who found him like I did."

Clint stuck his head out and took a quick look around. He managed to pull it back in again just ahead of a volley of gunshots fired from multiple directions. "They're not Hank's boys."

"Then that means we're in trouble, right?" Phoebe asked.

"Yeah," Clint replied. "We're in trouble."

THIRTY-NINE

Clint took a few shots out the door just to test the waters. It turned out the water was plenty hot and he immediately reloaded his gun.

"What are we going to do?" Phoebe asked, doing a good job of keeping calm.

Andy was outside in plain sight. Although he sported a swollen jaw and a bruised face, he still acted like he was cock of the walk. Strutting back and forth, he fired his gun at the cabin. "Yeah, Adams!" Andy shouted. "What're you gonna do now?"

Phoebe glared out at the young man as if she meant to take him on herself. "That little bastard," she hissed. "He'd be crying like a baby if all them others hadn't showed up."

Too wrapped up in his own bluster, Andy kept strutting and kept firing at the shack. "You gonna come out or do you want me to come in there myself?"

Clint kept low while moving to one of the cabin's dirty windows. He couldn't see everything through the smeared glass pane, but he could see enough to know that there wasn't much time left. "We need to get out of here," Clint said. "They're surrounding us."

"How many?" Phoebe asked.

"Can't tell, but the longer we wait, the worse it'll be."
Turning to look Phoebe in the eyes, he said, "Stay here and
keep your head down."

"Please don't leave me, Clint."

"Don't worry. I'll be right back."

Although Clint would never have said it to Phoebe, he
knew well enough that they were going to be hurt if they
stayed put. He also knew that things wouldn't be any
worse for her if he stepped out that door and didn't make it
back in.

When Clint did stand up and step out of the cabin, he
put thoughts of Phoebe or anything else aside. This was a
matter of survival. In the bigger picture, it was a matter of
testing the mettle of the gang he and Ossutt were up
against.

"Well, well," Andy sneered as he took a step back and
squared off against Clint. "Looks like The Gunsmith has
some balls, after all."

Clint didn't take the bait. "You're in over your head,
boy."

"Oh, really?"

"Don't worry about it. You're not the first to make that
mistake." Now that he was outside, Clint could see the
other gunmen moving forward. To them, he said, "You
won't be the last."

For the moment, they held their fire so they could see
what Clint had in mind. Most men who went up against
Clint would rather have it known that they bested him in
something close to a fair fight. Although Clint didn't much
like to concern himself with assholes like that, he sometimes used their line of thinking to his advantage.

For the moment, Clint's strategy was working fine. The
others were stepping up. Either they were waiting for their
moment of glory or they were too nervous to lift their guns
now that Clint had made it known that he wasn't afraid of
them.

Andy kept the arrogant smile on his face, but there wasn't so much confidence behind it anymore. Looking around to make sure the others were still there, he licked his lips and puffed out his chest. "You're outgunned."

"Then you want this to be one-on-one?"

The twitch on Andy's face was so bad that it looked like some sort of medical condition. His mind raced for something else to say, but couldn't come up with a damn thing. His eyes snapped back and forth to once again check that he had the others close by.

And then, without so much as a smart word, Andy lifted his gun to take aim.

A shot blasted through the air and echoed amid the barren trees. A single piece of lead punched through Andy's chest and knocked him off his feet. Both arms splayed out at the sides as he toppled straight back and landed with a solid thump against the ground. One last gust of steam rose from his mouth, taking the final spark of his life with it.

As soon as Clint pulled his trigger, his eyes had been looking for his next target. His round had landed right where he knew it would, leaving him free to decide which remaining man posed the most dangerous threat.

The one closest to Andy was startled by the shot that had killed the younger man and stepped back when he felt the warm spray of blood hit him. The other two had the opposite reaction and lifted their guns to give a violent reply to Clint's shot.

While shifting to aim at one of those two men, Clint dropped to one knee. The moment his knee touched against the frozen soil, the Colt in his hand barked twice in quick succession. Like the shot that had killed Andy, Clint placed these next two rounds like he was pointing to dots on a wall.

First one of the gunmen fell straight back as a hole was drilled through his forehead. Then, the second one jerked around in a tight spiral as hot lead caught him in the shoulder and pulled him back.

Other shots came from the surrounding trees and Clint responded to each one in turn. His mind didn't even bother with the bullets that whipped through the air inches from him. Worrying about them at this point in the game was senseless.

He was either going to win this fight or not.

Live or die.

There was no other alternative.

The firing was already starting to subside thanks to the men that had been taken down. One shot clipped Clint's shoulder, but only chewed up a section of his thick leather jacket. Clint's reaction was to shift his aim in that direction and pull his trigger.

When the man who'd fired at him started to move from his spot, he suddenly became easier to see. With his target in sight, Clint took another shot which hit the gunman squarely in the upper chest.

Now the firing was dwindling even more. Adding to that echo of thunder was the sound of footsteps crunching wildly against the ground, heading away from the cabin.

Clint stood up at the same time that one of the other gunmen got to his feet. This fellow had been knocked down earlier and the front of his coat was blackened by his own blood.

"You gonna leave or do you want some more?" Clint asked.

The man took half a second to think and then made his decision. His hand started to come up, but only made it a quarter of the way before Clint fired his last round. The bullet finished off the gunman, adding a fresh hole about an inch away from the first one.

Clint opened the cylinder of the Colt, dumped out the spent shells and replaced them with fresh ones from his gun belt. He snapped the pistol shut and looked around to see if any of the gunmen were still around.

Apart from the sound of horses galloping away, the only

thing to reach Clint's ears was the rustling of the wind. He then turned to the cabin and holstered the Colt.

"Phoebe?" Clint called out. "Are you all right?"

Eventually, the blonde peeked out from the cabin. Once she got a look at Clint, she jumped out from where she'd been hiding and raced into his arms. Her dress was still open, and her bare breasts were pressed against him.

"Oh, Clint, I've never seen anything like that," she gasped as she buried her face against Clint's chest. "I've never been so frightened."

"You did real good back there," he said as soothingly as he could. "But it's not over yet."

FORTY

Hank stomped into his study with his most trusted hands following him. They were the men who'd been with him the longest and proven themselves enough to gain the man's trust. Mace and Kyle were there, albeit wounded to various degrees. Zeke was winded but not hurt, and was the last of the hands to be allowed into the room at that moment.

"What happened while you were gone?" Hank asked in a tone that made it seem like he really didn't want to hear the answer. "What happened to Clint?"

Zeke made sure that nobody else was close enough to hear when he said, "Clint's fine." Seeing that Hank was about to let out a noise, Zeke held out his hands to keep him quiet. "Me and him split up on our way back so he could move about without being followed. I was supposed to come in and make sure there were not plenty of others around when I said that he was gone."

"That's why you wanted to be certain it was only us in here now," Mace said with a nod. "Sneaky, but I like it."

Kyle winced, but tried to act as though he felt no pain whatsoever. Mostly, he was tired after going without sleep for the last few days. "Why the trick?"

"Because we know that there's a spy around here and if

160

we let it be known that Clint's gone, them Reapers won't be looking for him later. Have you heard anything from Will Dreyer, Mr. Ossutt?"

Hank nodded and filled Zeke in on what had happened while he and Clint were away.

"Then we made it back just in time," Zeke said after Hank was through with his account.

"Hopefully, it was worth the trip all the way to some ghost town and back," Mace grunted. "Because we sure as hell could have used you two here."

"It was worth it," Zeke replied. "No doubt about that."

"What did you find in Ambling Creek?" Kyle asked.

Hearing the name of that town sent another chill through Zeke's body that had nothing to do with the winter's cold. Rather than bring up the subject of his missing uncle and cousins, Zeke took a breath and pushed those memories to the back of his mind. "First of all, we found out that anything you might have heard about these Reapers ain't just rumor. They're for real, Mr. Ossutt."

"I know that already," Hank said grimly.

"They'll come through here and take everything there is. As far as we could tell, most of 'em will approach in a group like a wave. Clint and I figured that much by looking at the tracks that was left. They'll be shooting and raising hell all along the way.

"Near as we could figure, there had to be about a dozen or so of them. The ones that aren't in that first wave will be waiting on the other side until the first one's done."

"Done with what?" Mace asked.

The expression on Zeke's face was dark as a moonless night. "Just about all the tracks we found led in one direction. Thank God for the cold because any warmer time of year, and there wouldn't be no tracks left. And there wasn't just footprints. There was blood, bullet holes, all around the prints, and they clumped all in one spot on the other side of town."

Slowly, Kyle started to nod. "Like they were being herded into one spot."

"That's what Clint said."

In response to the questioning glances he was seeing, Kyle explained, "It's a pincers maneuver. They've been teaching it at West Point since the Revolution. Gather the enemy into a strategic place and then close in on them from two sides."

"That's where the second wave came in," Zeke said. "The tracks from that group were easier to spot because they came in through side streets and met up outside of a storehouse. There was enough bullet holes, empty shells and blood to know that that was where the folks of Ambling Creek made their stand."

Hank was nodding and pacing the room. His eyes were wide and not focused on anything in front of him, but rather on what was going on inside his head. "So now we know how these killers work. Maybe we can come up with a way to use that to our advantage."

"Clint had some ideas about that, too," Zeke said. "And we'd best start working on them before it's too late. Considering what we found inside that storehouse, we shouldn't even be wasting more time standing around talking about it."

"What was in there?" Mace asked.

Zeke's face darkened as he thought about his family that had lived in Ambling Creek. "Bodies," he said. "Nothing but bodies."

FORTY-ONE

Eclipse carried Clint and Phoebe away from the rickety shack and into the outer acres of Ossutt's property. Clint steered directly for a spot that put him between the house and the spot where the Reapers were gathering. He then climbed down from the saddle and helped Phoebe down after him.

"This is the spot," he said. "We won't be found here."

"Are you sure about that?"

"Yeah. I caught Andy here and he wasn't spotted by Hank's or Dreyer's scouts. It took me a while before I was even able to find it."

Phoebe looked around. The land was uneven, but relatively flat. It sloped up into a bluff that wasn't even high enough to keep them from being picked out on the horizon. Finally, she looked over to Clint and asked, "Find what?"

But Clint wasn't there. In fact, not even Eclipse was there. Before she called out for him, Phoebe saw part of the side of the nearby bluff lift up like a trapdoor.

"Find this," Clint said from underneath the trapdoor.

It looked as though Clint was standing inside the bluff itself. Phoebe could hardly believe her eyes until she studied where he was standing while walking up to him.

The bluff actually was barely more than a gentle slope. Part of it had been dug out like a large notch cut into the earth. The other part of it was a simple wooden frame with planks connected to it. On top of the planks was a canvas cover beneath a layer of sod and leaves. A thick tangle of thorny bushes lay around the hideaway, presumably to keep anyone from riding too close to it.

All in all, it was like stepping into the confidence of a magician. Once Phoebe got close enough to see how the trick was done, she wondered how it was that everyone else hadn't figured it out.

Eclipse was already laying with his legs tucked close to his body, but there was still enough room for the stallion to stand up if need be. He wouldn't have been able to lift his head, but the possibility was there. As for Clint and Phoebe, there was more than enough room for them to hunker down and lower the trapdoor back into place.

The door shut with a thump, making the buried structure seem more like a cave. The only light that penetrated the protective cover trickled in from between some leaves. A larger beam shone in through slits that had been cut in the front and back.

Clint settled in with his back against the earthen wall. "If I had to guess, I'd say this is where Andy slept when everyone was out looking for him."

Rummaging in one corner of the enclosed space, Phoebe found a bundle wrapped in what looked to be a tablecloth. "And it looks like he meant to spend some more time in here as well." She held up the bundle and opened it to reveal some strips of beef jerky and a hunk of bread that was almost hard enough to knock a nail into a wall.

"Hand that over," Clint said. "I'm hungry enough for that to look appetizing."

Phoebe brought the bundle of food with her as she crawled over and sat with her back against his chest. After pulling off a hunk of bread for herself, she handed the rest to Clint. "How long should we stay in here?"

Reaching out with one hand, Clint pushed aside some of the leaves that covered the slit in the wall directly in front of him. "See them?" he asked, pointing outside.

It took a moment or two of squinting, but Phoebe spotted what Clint was showing her. Through the slit, she could see all the way across to the fence line. Waiting there, like a row of crows perched on a telegraph wire, were five riders. As she watched, another rider came up to join the group.

"I see them," she said.

"Those are the men who've been leading the ambushes. When they're ready, they'll head out of there."

"And you mean to surprise them from here?"

"Not hardly. We barely made it out of one tight spot. There's no sense in letting ourselves get cornered into an even tighter one. We'll wait for them to pass and then follow them. Hopefully, Zeke's made it back to make sure Hank knows what to do. If it works, we might be able to beat these men at their own game."

"But there's so many of them."

"If it works the way I hope it does, the numbers won't matter."

"But how can you be certain about any of it? Have you ridden against these men before?"

"No, but I saw the kind of damage they do. I've gotten a look at how they work and how they fight." Clint could tell that Phoebe was getting frightened by what he was saying. "It's like when you're playing a game against someone," he said, shifting his language to something less threatening. "Once you see how someone wins, you get an idea of how you can beat them."

Her muscles relaxed a bit and she took a bite of bread. "That's pretty simple."

"The easier the better, as long as it works."

"So how long do you think we'll be here?"

"When all those horses start moving, we'll hear them. Also, I'm pretty sure they'll be making plenty of noise. Until we hear that or see them moving, we'll just have to sit tight."

Nestling in against him, Phoebe shifted so she was laying with one shoulder on Clint's chest. She slipped one hand behind him and laid the other over his torso. "You think it might take a while?"

Clint could feel his body responding to her touch. That response grew when her hand started working its way below his belt. "Could be a while, but we need to be ready to move."

"Then we shouldn't waste any time." With that, Phoebe turned around so that she was laying on top of him. A few more shifts and she was straddling Clint with her legs curled on either side of him. "I thought I was dead back in that cabin. Now I feel more alive than ever. I don't want that feeling to stop just yet."

FORTY-TWO

Clint wriggled out of his coat and draped it over Phoebe's back like a makeshift blanket. Since she was on top of him, they were both covered and sheltered from what little wind actually made it into the hidden room. The fact of the matter was that the coat was hardly necessary since their bodies were making more than enough heat to keep them warm.

The sound of the distant riders gathering was a constant rumble in Clint's ears. He did his best to keep at least part of his mind focused on that since the rest of him was being pleasantly distracted by Phoebe's wandering hands.

She unbuckled his pants and slipped them down just far enough for her to reach in and stroke his growing erection. A wide smile spread across her face as she felt Clint's hands slip under her skirts and rub against the smooth skin of her thighs.

Even though he couldn't see her naked skin, feeling it was more than enough to put a smile onto Clint's face. He closed his eyes and leaned back, tracing the supple line of her hips and buttocks with the palms of his hands. In no time at all, both of them were so warm that they forgot about the wintry chill swirling all around them.

Every now and then, Phoebe would start to make a noise, but held herself back. She could hear the riders gathering in the distance as well and didn't want to push their luck by exposing their hiding spot. And when she forced herself to remain silent, it made the pleasure she was feeling all the more intense.

She was leaning forward now, her blond hair spilling down to cover her and Clint's faces at the same time. Phoebe's lips opened slightly and pressed against Clint's. Their tongues slipped out to greet each other, and when their kiss became more passionate, she started moaning softly.

The sound was something close to a purr. Clint listened to it grow louder as he placed one hand over her backside and used the other to guide his cock between her legs. He soon found the hot dampness of her pussy and pulled her down onto him.

Phoebe slid along the length of his rigid penis, shuddering as she took more and more of it inside of her. When she felt that he was all the way in, Phoebe moved both hands over his chest, up along his shoulders, and then slipped her fingers through his hair.

From there, she started rocking back and forth. Their bodies came together in a way that made her forget about everything that had happened. For those moments, she didn't worry about anything but where he was touching her and how she might hold back from calling out his name for everyone to hear.

Clint shifted his back against the earthen wall, holding onto Phoebe so he could take her with him as he lowered himself onto the floor. Once they were both laying on the ground, Clint took hold of the coat and pulled it tight against her so that she was laying on it when he rolled her onto her back.

Phoebe's skirts were bunched around her waist and draped over them both as she wrapped one leg around him.

Their bodies and clothes were entwined like a cocoon around them. Their breath was coming in shorter, heavier gasps as Clint began pumping harder in and out of her.

Sliding his hands up over her ample breasts, Clint kept them moving until he was tracing a line over both of her arms, which ended with his fingers threading between hers. Holding her hands tightly, Clint held her to the ground as he rose up slightly above her.

Phoebe arched her back and opened her legs wider to accommodate him. Her eyes snapped open as she watched his muscles straining with every thrust. Finally, Clint hit that perfect spot inside of her that sent a jolt of pleasure through her.

Phoebe arched her back and trembled with her approaching climax. Clint could feel the eruption welling up inside of her and knew that she was going to let out a groan that would shake the trapdoor over their heads.

Clint thrust all the way inside of her while leaning down to press his lips solidly against Phoebe's mouth. That combination caused her to grab hold of him so tightly that it seemed she was holding on for dear life. She did let out a noise, but most of it passed straight from her to him.

The ground beneath them started to tremble as a distant thunder reached Clint's ears. That brought his head snapping up so he could look toward the slit in the wall.

"They're starting to move," Clint whispered.

Phoebe sat up a bit so she could get a look toward that narrow little window as well. "How long before we need to follow them?"

"I figure we should give them a bit of a head start. Without that, they might spot us as we're coming out of here."

Clint could feel her body shifting against him. Phoebe's hips lifted a bit off the ground so she could slide his cock in and out of her.

His heart pounded in his chest and he allowed himself to feed the hunger that was growing in him. Clint looked back down to Phoebe and saw that she was gazing up at him expectantly. Her eyes grew wide as he lowered himself onto her once more and thrust eagerly between her legs.

The momentary break didn't curb their passion in the least. Once Clint buried his penis inside of her a few more times, they were both within seconds of climax. She wrapped her arms around him and held on tighter than ever as her orgasm pulsed through her body.

Clint dug his hand under her skirt to feel the creamy skin of her thigh as he exploded inside of her. The climax worked its way under both of their skins, leaving them breathless. Despite the cold in the rest of the outside world, Clint and Phoebe were sweating.

When she opened her eyes, Phoebe no longer looked scared. She didn't look worried, and she didn't even seem concerned with the outlaw riders gathering in the distance. She placed one hand on Clint's cheek and kissed him gently.

"Thank you," she whispered.

"No need for that. I feel like I can step outside and take on an army."

Judging by the rumble building up in the ground, it seemed that Clint might just have to put that feeling to the test.

FORTY-THREE

Outside, the horses were still galloping toward the fence. Soon, the sound of splintering wood filled the air. By the time the Reapers galloped onto Ossutt's property, Clint and Phoebe were watching them through the slit in the wall of their hiding spot.

Eclipse was shifting nervously in his corner of the enclosed space, sensing the other horses which weren't too far away.

"How many of them do you see?" Phoebe asked.

"Hard to make out with the sun right behind them. No doubt that's how they planned it. Even so, I'd say there's at least ten of them."

She shuddered and looked away from the slit. "Sounds like a lot more than that."

"Horses can be mighty noisy when their riders want it that way. Also, don't forget we're laying against the ground right now. That's going to make it seem like they're right on top of us."

As soon as those words came out of Clint's mouth, the rumble from the approaching horses became even louder. Phoebe covered her ears, but that didn't do any good since

171

she was pressed against the same ground that was being punished by all those hooves.

Even Clint winced under the ruckus. He could see that the riders would come close to the hiding place, but would steer clear of it by at least fifteen to twenty yards.

The riders weren't in any sort of formation. Instead, they spread out like a raggedy blanket. The only sign of organization was the pair of horses at the front of the entire group. Those two faced straight ahead, as if they could already see the faces of the men waiting for them at the ranch house. All the others were hollering and tearing up the ground beneath their horses' hooves. Clearly, this was the moment they'd all been waiting for.

Once the group of riders passed by, Clint moved to the other side of the enclosed space so he could look through the slit on the opposite wall. With the sun at their backs, it was much easier for the individual riders to be picked out.

"Are they gone?" Phoebe asked meekly.

"They've moved on, but they're not gone. Looks like there's not quite as many of them as I thought."

"After what happened with Andy, there's less of them still breathing."

Phoebe had a point. In fact, Clint thought back to the other times that he and the Reapers had traded lead. Each of those times, it had been the outlaws who'd come up short.

"All right," Clint said after the riders' thunder had started to recede. "Time to get moving."

"What about me?" Phoebe asked.

"You'll stay here and wait for me to come back for you. I can't think of anyplace safer."

"What if someone finds me here?"

"I wouldn't worry about that. With all that's going to happen at the house, I doubt anyone'll have the time to comb the hills for this place."

Although there was still strength in Phoebe's eyes, Clint

could also see some fear trickling in around the edges. He held her chin in one hand and used the other to push away some hair that had fallen into her face. "If I'm not back for you by midnight, then work your way back to the house and don't show yourself to anyone you don't recognize."

"All right," she said reluctantly.

Clint reached back to where Eclipse was scraping anxiously at the ground. He removed the rifle which he kept slung in a holster on his saddle. "Take this," Clint said as he handed her the rifle. "If the time comes, don't hesitate to use it. Understand?"

She nodded. Once she got her hands on the rifle, Phoebe tightened her grip on the weapon and nodded once more. This time, the strength in her eyes was doing a good job of pushing back the fear. "I understand."

Clint kept his eyes on her until he knew that she was strong enough. After that, he just took a moment to enjoy the sight of her. "I'll be back for you. I promise."

"I know you will."

Once Clint stepped away from her, he immediately went to Eclipse and got the Darley Arabian ready to ride. The stallion was born to run, so those preparations took less than a minute or two. After that, Clint pushed back the trapdoor and led Eclipse into the open.

The door fit right back into place, and even though he knew it was there, Clint had a hard time picking out the shape of the structure he'd just left. Knowing that Phoebe was safe, he climbed into the saddle and flicked the reins.

Eclipse dug his hooves into the dirt and took off like he'd been shot from a gun barrel.

FORTY-FOUR

"You hear that?" Kyle asked as he squinted into the distance.

Next to him, Mace spat onto the ground and shifted in his saddle. "Yeah, I hear just fine. It's about damn time those assholes finally got moving."

Both men sat on their horses with their backs to the cluster of buildings including the ranch house. Compared to how noisy it had been at the Double Briar for the last few days, the silence in the air now was getting almost too thick to bear.

"Are all the men called in?" Kyle asked.

Mace let out a grunting laugh. "You mean them patrols? They're back, for all the good they did. Seems like nobody saw anything or did much out there anyhow."

"It gave the men something to do while we waited."

"Waited for what?"

"For right here and now." As Kyle said that, he straightened up and extended a finger to the open prairie ahead of him. "There they are."

Mace pulled the shotgun from the holster on his saddle and checked to make sure it was loaded. Snapping the shotgun closed with a flick of his wrist, he pulled his horse around and said, "I'll spread the word."

Kyle nodded. Although he'd signed on as a rancher all those years ago as a way to avoid a life spent spilling blood, he knew there was a time when such things were necessary. Now that it was here, he was glad to get it over with one way or another.

Drawing the pistol from its holster, Kyle took hold of his reins and moved his horse away from the fence surrounding the house. Already, he could hear the sounds of the other men saddling up and riding out to meet him.

"Remember," Ossutt shouted as he pulled on a coat and stepped down from the front porch of his house. "I don't want you men to take a shot unless you have to. And if it comes to that, remember the plan."

The ranch hands nodded and looked out toward the horizon where the riders where approaching. Even though most of them thought they were ready for this, they felt their confidence starting to fray around the edges.

The Reapers were coming, and it was plain to see that they were in no mood for bargaining.

Will Dreyer rode out at the front of his men like a general leading an army. Although his own army had lost a few members, the ones that remained had no trouble remembering who they were.

The horses had carried them straight across the open acres of Ossutt's land like a plow cutting through wet soil. There was nobody standing in their way. By the looks of it, all of the ranchers were gathered around their houses waiting for them.

None of that would matter.

Dreyer had seen it all before. He and his men would ride through them and then take what they wanted.

"All right, boys!" he shouted. "Take down whoever don't run. Them that do run, make sure we get 'em in the right place! This is our ranch now, Reapers! Let's claim it!"

Dreyer's words echoed among the pounding of the

horses' hooves. The rest of the gang let out a holler of their own as they started firing into the air and digging their heels into their horses' sides. Even the animals became enraged, and their eyes turned wild as the foam came to their mouths.

The ranch house had started off as a speck in the distance. Now it was growing larger by the second, until finally the Reapers began knocking down the rails or riding straight over them.

A few gunshots started popping here and there in front of Dreyer and his men, but none of those bullets came close to hitting anything. Instead, they seemed more like panicked fire that was getting squeezed off while someone was running in the other direction.

Dreyer grinned to himself. Although he was always pleased to see things happen just as he'd predicted, it was a wonder how folks could all be so cowardly in exactly the same way. Just like all the ranches and all the towns before the Double Briar, this one was going to fall like a load of bricks.

Lifting his own gun, Dreyer took aim at the first fleeing person he could find and pulled his trigger. That part was always fun.

FORTY-FIVE

Clint was sitting in the saddle with his body low over Eclipse's neck. He'd pushed the Darley Arabian to his limits, hoping to get around the main group of riders in a short amount of time. The stallion had never let him down before and he certainly didn't now.

Eclipse charged over the frozen ground with ease. Although he slipped a bit every now and then, his footing was sure enough that he didn't come close to falling. In fact, the only problem from Clint's point of view was the fact that his face was catching one hell of a chill after cutting through so much freezing wind.

In no time at all, he'd circled around the cluster of buildings in the middle of the ranch and was coming around toward the back. He had no trouble seeing or hearing the main group of Reapers charging over the front gate. Clint kept moving past them, however, until he was facing the back section of prairie.

I sure hope I'm right about this, he thought.

For a moment, Clint saw nothing but empty ground between himself and the rest of the property. The house and stable were at his back, and just when he was about to turn around and head in that direction, he saw exactly what he'd been hoping to see.

The sight of the second group of Reapers was hardly a good one, but it was most definitely welcome just then. According to what they'd seen in Ambling Creek, Clint and Zeke had pieced together the Reapers' strategy of closing in on their target from two directions. It was a practical and very effective tactic which had served them well enough before. Clint's gamble had been that the Reapers would use that same strategy this time around.

Sure enough, the second group was coming in from the opposite end of the property, headed straight for the back of the house. Clint steered Eclipse toward them and gave the reins and extra snap.

One of the Reapers spotted him in seconds and paused a moment to get a look at his face. By the time Clint was picked out as someone not in the gang, the riders closest to him had turned their guns in his direction. Clint waited until he got the twitch in the back of his head that always told him he was quickly running out of time to defend himself. Before that time ran out, Clint picked a target and sent a bullet in his direction.

The shot cracked through the air and caused one of the riders to twist a bit in his saddle. Other shots sounded, and soon Clint heard lead whipping through the air on either side. Rather than start firing any faster, Clint caused Eclipse to weave back and forth while he tried to take careful aim at each of his targets.

Once he got used to the constant motion, Clint started firing again and quickly dropped two of the riders from their saddles. The men hit the ground hard and rolled in heaps upon it. Once the weight from their saddles had been taken away, the horses picked their own direction and split off before making it to the fence.

The rider at the front of the smaller group shouted an obscenity in Clint's direction and started firing like a madman. His eyes blazed with an angry fire as he sent shot after shot in a pattern that was bound to hit Clint before too long.

Clint put an end to those shots with one of his own. The modified Colt blasted once and sent a round through the air to punch a hole through the rider's skull. The other man snapped back and dropped from his saddle as if he was tied to the wrong end of a short rope.

Seeing three of their companions drop in a matter of seconds, the remaining couple of riders started glancing nervously among themselves. The group hadn't been too big at the start and it was even smaller now.

Clint could feel the fear coming off the others and decided to give them one more push in the right direction. Taking aim, he squeezed his trigger and sent a bullet so close to one of the others' head that it knocked the hat clean off of him.

That was more than enough to send that one in another direction, and the remaining two riders were close behind them. The men fired wildly over their shoulders, quickly emptying their guns to cover their escape.

Clint smirked to himself, knowing that he'd already taken a big piece out of Will Dreyer's attack. As much as he wanted to chase down and capture those escaping Reapers, Clint turned Eclipse toward the ranch house and snapped the reins.

The Darley Arabian cleared the fence with inches to spare and hit the ground running. It wasn't difficult to figure out where the rest of the Reapers were. All Clint needed to do was follow the sound of gunshots.

FORTY-SIX

"They're runnin'!" Beeman shouted as he fired a shot toward one of the ranch hands fleeing in front of him.

Dreyer smiled and replied, "Of course they are! Herd them into the stable. Looks like they're already headed that way, so let's make sure they don't make it out."

Beeman gave Dreyer a nod and fired a few more times at the ranchers on foot.

Although the ranchers hadn't been on horseback, they knew the ground much better and had started fleeing before the Reapers had cleared the fence. No bodies were on the ground just yet, but they all knew that was set to change before too long.

The wide front door to the stable opened, allowing a stream of panicked cowboys, and even Hank Ossutt himself, to flee for their lives. Dreyer was hot on their tails, looking around for the second wave of Reapers who were responsible for bringing up the rear. Of course, with the ranchers willingly diving for cover, the second wave wasn't much needed.

Once he got a few paces closer to the stables where everyone was hiding, Dreyer got a feeling in the pit of his stomach. It was the thrill of the chase, drawn to its in-

evitable climax. It was the expectation of all the blood that
was to be shed.

It was the excitement that always came right before
victory.

Or maybe it was the sensation of slipping across a sheet
of ice.

In an instant, Dreyer was snapped out of his silent
reverie when he realized that his horse was kicking and
skidding over a patch of frozen ground. In fact, every one
of his men were skidding as well.

And it wasn't just a patch of ground, but an entire section of it covered with a thick layer of mostly frozen water
surrounding the stable. The sound of ice cracking gave way
to the wet sloshing of hooves slipping against wet earth.

As he toppled forward, Dreyer felt as if he was drifting
slowly to the ground. His wide eyes soaked up everything
in front of him: the shallow trench dug into the ground, the
water inside it and the crust of ice frozen on top. He even
caught a glimpse of the narrow, perfectly dry footpath leading into the stable.

Then Dreyer's chin hit the ground and his horse slammed
right down beside him. In fact, every last one of the Reapers
slipped and fell into a heap. Those that tried to steer clear of
the ice were simply tripped up by those who'd been caught
in the trap.

Trap.

That word flew into Dreyer's mind even as the pain
from his broken bones started to take hold of him.

Several seconds of noisy chaos turned into a low rumble
of pained grunts coming from both animal and gunman
alike. Soon, the sound of the stable doors being pushed
open filled the night.

"What the hell . . . ?" Dreyer grunted. Straining to look
over his shoulder at his men, he screamed, "What the hell
are you waiting for?! Shoot these bastards!"

"You're not shooting anyone," Clint said as he rode

around the stable. Looking down at the ice-covered moat surrounding the building, he said, "Not a bad job considering the amount of time you had."

Hank stepped out of the stable, flanked by Mace, Kyle, Zeke and several more of his workers. Every one of them were carrying guns. "Nothin' but some elbow grease, shovels and one hell of a cold night. Oh, and I'd say your trip to Ambling Creek had something to do with it."

Dreyer blinked at the sound of that. The name of the town seemed to ring a bell with him, but it wasn't anything he could quite wrap his mind around. Shaking off the fog settling into his head, he gritted his teeth and struggled to get to his feet. He made it up to one knee before he realized that his other leg was broken.

"This . . . place . . . is mine," Dreyer grunted. "Ain't no . . . fucking rancher gonna . . . run me away. You're dead."

Clint could see the look in Dreyer's eyes. It was the same look that was in the eyes of all the Reapers. "Toss away your guns and we'll take you to the law," Clint said, noticing that a bunch of the gunmen were getting to their feet. "This can all end right here."

Beeman was the one to answer that statement as he straightened up and snarled, "You're damn right it ends here."

The moment Beeman lifted his gun, every one of the Reapers who was able followed his lead. Their hands raised to aim at any of the people in front of them. Before one of the Reapers could pull his trigger, they were cut down in a hailstorm of lead which came from the stables.

Shotguns, rifles, pistols, hunting guns and even a modified Colt lent their voices to the barrage. When the smoky thunder cleared, the only things drawing breath in front of that stable were a few of the fallen horses.

"I suppose you're moving on," Hank said when he saw Clint flicking Eclipse's reins.

"Not just yet. I need to bring back one of your workers."

Hank's eyes lit up. "You found Percy?"

"Yeah. And once she's back, I'll be staying on for a little while. There's some fences that need to be repaired."

Hank stepped forward, smoking shotgun cradled in his arm, and looked down at the dead, gaping face of Will Dreyer. "Like the Good Book says: 'Even as I have seen, those who plow iniquity and sow trouble reap the same.'"

"There's plenty of good words in that book," Clint said as he leaned forward and took a peek inside the stable. When he spotted Lynne cowering nearby, he said, "Something about honoring thy father springs to mind."

Her face was stained with tears and all the fire had gone out of her eyes. Clint knew that if this night hadn't shown her the error of her ways, nothing would.

Watch for

THE DEADLY AND THE DIVINE

288th novel in the exciting GUNSMITH series
from Jove

Coming in December!

J. R. ROBERTS

THE GUNSMITH

GIANT ACTION! GIANT ADVENTURE!

THE GUNSMITH

GIANT

GIANT WESTERNS FEATURING THE GUNSMITH

THE GHOST OF BILLY THE KID
0-515-13622-0

LITTLE SURESHOT AND THE WILD WEST SHOW
0-515-13851-7

DEAD WEIGHT
0-515-14028-7

AVAILABLE WHEREVER BOOKS ARE SOLD OR AT PENGUIN.COM

J799

LONGARM

Explore the exciting Old West with one of the men who made it wild!

AVAILABLE WHEREVER BOOKS ARE SOLD OR AT PENGUIN.COM

(Ad # B112)

TODAY'S HOTTEST ACTION WESTERN!